THE SEX CULT MURDERS

by

I0638435

CHARLES NUETZEL

WRITING AS "FRED MACDONALD"

The Borgo Press
An Imprint of Wildside Press

MMVII

Copyright © 1965, 2007 by Charles Nuetzel
Originally published under the pseudonym, Fred
MacDonald

All rights reserved.
No part of this book may be reproduced in any form
without the expressed written consent
of the author and publisher.
Printed in the United States of America

SECOND EDITION

CONTENTS

INTRODUCTION

The hard-boiled detective has been a literary standard for decades, reaching a highpoint with Mickey Spillane's Mike Hammer in the 1950s. I never met Spillane, although I shared an autograph session with him at a trade show—I mention this simply because Spillane died this week.

What I recall most of the Hammer books was how the ladies flocked to his standard, at which point he'd turn into a wild man, slam on his hat (those were the days!), and go rushing out of the place with his tail on fire. All of this seemed great to a young reader, although it was pretty tame stuff by today's standards.

His books inspired me to develop several hard-boiled mysteries of my own during the early and mid-1960s. *The Sex Cult Murders* was my third such venture, if I recall correctly.

The writing was a voyage of discovery—I had no better idea of the outcome when I started than the reader did. As the tale developed, I learned where it was going when the characters moved in that direction, and discovered the solution to the mystery just before my fans did.

A plot line runs across the pages of a book. You start with a premise, and you see where it takes you. I always had a pretty good idea of the wordage with which I was allowed to work (paperback publishers in those days had very strict size limitations), and I tried to pace the story accordingly.

But the final climax where the hero and bad guy (note that I'm being PC here!) clash for the last time in a life-and-death struggle—well, that was a mystery until right up to the very end. I gave my hero the lead, and he ran with it, asking questions and pushing witnesses until he (and I) got some answers.

So blame it all on Mickey Spillane and Mike Hammer!

—Charles Nuetzel
Thousand Oaks, California
July 2006

CHAPTER I.

I have an attitude about life that isn't necessarily original in itself, but which generally has kept me going for thirty-one years, some of them in Korea, some in the jungles of the cement civilization in which I make my living as a part-time business operator and part-time private detective: Don't ask questions, act first!

Most men in my profession would attempt to make everybody believe that they are God's gift to women, and women throw themselves at them like moths chase lights. In my case, I've had my share of broads; all kinds. But don't think I'm some guy who has his pick. But there are enough.

That's how the *Harryington Murder Case* started. With a woman.

I had known Linda some years before, when I was just out of the service. I'd been bumming around Lake Arrowhead, a summer vacation resort some sixty or so miles from Los Angeles, when I met her. It was one of those relationships that had developed fast into a raging romance. Several facts got into our way, including her father and by the end

7

of summer the affair had been simmered slightly down. We had split friends, with the promise to meet again sometime. But it didn't happen. Usually that is the end of most relationships; you promise to meet again, and never do. It might have happened with her, only we lost contact—her long stay out of the country simply ended things completely.

Linda was stacked like most society dames don't like to admit to as being the norm—for society ladies, that is. She was all sexual energy; with the curves in the right places, and there were plenty of them!

Linda was twenty-seven when I bumped into her in a Beverly Hills cocktail lounge, a few months ago. She was sitting at the bar, sipping a Whiskey Sour. At first I actually didn't recognize her; all I noticed was a very neat rear-end view of a very attractive fanny.

She was dressed in a black silk sheath that hugged her buttocks like the standard layer of skin. I hate clichés, but sometime there's no other way of telling the facts. What I could see of her flaming red hair and figure, gave me the kind of thoughts a man gets while watching a stripper dancing through the climax of her act.

I'd just finished an investigation for a rich husband who had had every right to believe his wife was sleeping out on him. A good hunk of the three thousand dollar fee was still in my wallet and I'd decided it was time to take a short vacation from the reality of the everyday hell that the civilized jungle has become. It was an old habit of mine. Once a case was closed, it was time for a good old-fashion blast.

Linda's voluptuous backside view fired the obvious. She looked like the kind of woman that had come out for the evening to find a man. My mission in life had always been to help women find men! Me.

When the cocktail waitress came for my order I asked her to offer a drink to the lady at the bar. Once pointed out to the waitress, she stepped over to Linda and made my offer.

Linda turned, looked at him. Frowned. She had large, dark eyes that had a hauntingly sad look about them. Her lips were full, dimpled at the corners, giving them a pouting appearance; very delightful for kissing exercises. Her large, thrusting breasts pushed out the front of her low cut dress, revealing full supple white flesh. She looked at me more closely and then smiled.

It was then that I recognized her.

Right from where she was she stood, said:

"Stan Maxton!" Then she was in the booth with me, hands gripping mine. "God, you don't know how good it is to see you!"

For a long time we just looked at one another, like lost children. I could hardly believe my eyes. The emotions that had raced our summer romance to a frantic climax welled up through me like a tornado. All I could think of was here she was the only girl that I'd given a damned about! Well, that kind of summer adventure can be very meaningful. There had been other women, delightful ones, but she was special.

"Linda...how you been?" I said in a much more emotional voice than I'd intended.

"Fine...and you?"

"Bumming around," he said, avoiding her eyes.

"Still?"

"Well, actually I'm doing pretty well. In the private investigation business, pays good."

She gave me one of those smiles that curled my nerves tight. "Oh, Stan, you're a God-send for sore eyes. You don't know how much...well, you don't want to hear my problems. They're old ones, really."

I ordered a round of drinks and we sat there for several more moments, just looking at one another, silently thinking our own thoughts. In a way I couldn't decide if I was glad to see her, or not. What might it end?

"Still under the thumb?" I inquired.

She lowered her eyes. "In a way, Stan. You can't beat City Hall!"

"City Hall, hell! The Old Man, you mean!"

She nodded, then shook her head. "Let's get drunk as hell and celebrate!"

"What?"

"What you think? Meeting!"

The drinks came then, and we sipped them, talked about old times, about the summer that had given us so much pleasure and so much pain. Her father had been against our romance right from the start and had done everything he could to break up our romance. Luckily things had simmered out a bit by the time she was sent to Germany for a prolonged visit.

"Anything serious in the way of men?" I inquired, shakily. The very thought of her body embraced by another male animal sent slow chills down my spine. That was silly, but just a normal

10

male reaction concerning somebody he'd enjoyed so much. And she was something amazing, vibrant and lovely.

She shook her head. "Nothing serious, nothing like you and me. Just casual stuff."

Silence. We finished off the drinks and I ordered another round. By the time it had come, we were back in a lively conversation.

"I guess you get a lot of women in your line of business...a Mike Hammer, hammerin' away!" she teased, with a throaty laugh.

"No more than the average man stuff, my dear. That's the trouble with the public, they have this image of the private dick and think all girls, women and old ladies throw themselves around their necks. I do a job and get paid. Nothing more exciting than that. I blast out on a spree when a case is over, or when a contract has been signed on some promotional arrangement. That's another line of mine, but let's not talk about that. The thing is...the tension of my work calls for a little fun now and then."

"On a spree?" she asked.

"Just finished a case, if that's what you mean." She immediately asked about the case. I countered with: "Against company policy to talk about cases...private communications and all that junk. Legal baloney, sure. But damn if it doesn't sound impressive!"

We laughed; but it was the laughter of lovers who have rediscovered each other after a long time, the pleasure of remembering and the joy of knowing what will, in a short time, take place.

We were old lovers. We were single. And both of us out for an evening of pleasure. Just lucky to bump into one another and resolve that problem.

"How about us getting out of this dump?" Linda suggested. "I have a car down the street if you want to go someplace with me."

Her eyes twinkled, knowingly. That's the nice thing about friends, they have a past to fall back on, and the communication can be shortcut leaps through a lot of rubbish one has to go through with strangers or new acquaintances.

I paid for the drinks. Her car was parked a block away and was a little more fancy than I'd expected. Her family had money. I'd known that. But this was big money. I didn't recognize the make and asked about it.

"Custom built!" she explained with a happy edge of pride. "Always nice to have 'em build to match one's personal needs."

To me a car was designed to get from point A to point Z with the least amount of trouble.

The car was a sports model with bucket seats up front. Linda opened her purse and took out some keys, handing them to me. "Want to get in the driver's seat?"

"Like you better believe!"

She laughed as I opened the door for her. A moment later we were driving down Sunset Boulevard, toward the Pacific Ocean. Linda had suggested we head in that direction. For a long time we didn't talk. I was trapped up in my own whirling questions about Linda.

She had money; lots of it; that was obvious now. I wondered about her going to a bar and picking up some slob like myself; and surely, I reasoned, that was what she'd think of me, if she had all the money that the car and her words implied. Was she still a society dame on a spree; a rich man's daughter; or some guy's wife or mistress. All those roles would fit her; could be her. I wanted to ask the questions and get the answers, but somehow there just didn't seem a way to go about it without seeming too nosy. I mean. We had our time together back then, but everything else was a separate issue. That was her private domain and not for grabs unless she offered it up. And I wasn't about to ask. The only promise made, so far, was a night together, and remember old times. Linda was being closed-mouthed; if she didn't want me to know something, it wouldn't do any good asking.

Sunset Boulevard in Hollywood has, on the Strip, all the magic jazzy neat clubs. Then it blends out into the rich lands of Beverly Hills, and then goes through Bel Air and Brentwood, where the money-makers and status seekers live, mostly the latter, because no matter how much money a guy makes he makes it a habit of living ten thousand feet over his money level. After the Brentwood and the Country Clubs for rich status seekers, there comes the rolling, curving highway that cuts through the less expensive, but still plush, beach homes. Then finally the blue Pacific, which isn't always as blue as it is washed out gray blue.

The moon was full as we reached 101 Freeway, brightening up the ocean blackness that stretched out to infinity. Linda instructed that I go north.

"You have a place in mind?"

She grinned, but said nothing. She smoked silently, looking out through the windshield. We had driven about ten minutes when she said to turn right

13

at the next road off the highway. Once done, she gave me instructions to turn up a private roadway that led up into the cliffs overlooking the Pacific. Finally we came to a small, expensive looking beach house that extended over the edge of a downgrade on long steel stilts. It didn't look safe; but none of those kind of hillside houses does. She told me to park the car. We got out and stepped up to the darkened house.

"Your place?" I asked as she picked the right key and opened the door.

She nodded and stepped into the small hallway. I followed, closing the door behind me. A light switched on and I found myself looking into one of the slickest beach house living rooms that it's been my pleasure to see. There was wall to wall carpeting, off-white, thickly cushioned furniture, a small, conservative home bar and a large window that covered the full opposite wall, looking out across the ocean.

"Like?" she asked, turning and looking up at me. Her lips were half parted and she had the appearances of a little girl who had grown up into an extremely sexy woman.

"Like!" I exclaimed, resisting the impulse to kiss her.

"Let's have a drink, I'm dulled by the ride," she suggested, bouncing her way to the small home bar. "Let's have a bottle and blast off as you say!" She giggled and stepped around the bar.

"What'll it be, sir?" she asked, looking very grim.

"Make it Scotch!"

As she was pouring drinks, I found myself won-

14

dering again what kind of woman I'd gotten involved with this time. After all, we really didn't know one another like before. We were, pretty much strangers who had shared a short period of time when very young. Life had changed both of us. Her, especially. I began to wonder about Linda.

She handed me a glass full of Scotch and then came to my side.

"A little funnin', sir?" She squeezed my hand and kicked off her shoes. "Make yourself comfortable, I always say!" She pulled me to a sofa that faced the large window-wall. We sat down, close, so that our thighs were lightly touching. I put an arm around Linda's shoulder. It was the first physical contact of an intimate nature since we were kids. The effect was startling.

Linda was soft and yielding; she nestled against me, resting her head on my shoulder.

"You feel good," she murmured contentedly.

"Same goes for you, baby!" I squeezed her tighter against me. "What's the script call for now?"

She looked inquiringly up at me.

"Don't you like me? Don't you like the house? Don't you like the drink?" she asked, frowning.

"On the first two counts, yes—on the drink, I don't know." I tasted. It was good and I told her so.

"It should be. The most expensive we can get." She looked pleased; almost like a child who has managed to do the right thing for her parents.

Well, after a few drinks and light, pointless conversation, we somehow came together. I remember Linda suddenly slipping into my arms, her lips so soft and deliciously warm. All the passion that had been there before was even more sharply hungry now. She had matured beautifully. Then she moved back, smiling, confident in her total control of the situation. Well, at least that's how I remember it. The next thing I knew I was carrying her across the room.

"Down the hall," she murmured soft.

The door was open to her large bedroom. She directed me there and I kicked the door closed behind me and lay Linda on the large double bed. The room was oak-wood walled, the furniture, blonde colored and expensive looking, like everything else about Linda's little beach home.

But my eyes only made a quick sweep of the room, then returned to Linda.

She was already struggling out of her dress and I watched as she stripped it off and started to remove her bra.

"Honey, leave something for the man!" I managed to rasp, moving to her and starting to work on the straps of her bra while kissing the white hollow of her throat. She murmured and a tremor rushed over the flesh under my lips. Finally her bra fell free and she slipped her arms from the straps.

Her breasts were white ivory, firm and as youthful as I remember; the nipples were pink buds, erect and waiting for the heat of my kisses. My lips found the soft firm point on one breast as I leaned her back on the bed.

She was soft, trembling silk, hot and exciting, hungry for the caresses my hands and lips whispered over her body. She clawed at me during the last moments; her hands clamped me down against her arching body, which was straining up against me. The hours that followed were a heated mixture

16

of love making and conversation, which revealed nothing more about Linda, except that she thought I was better than she remembered. It was revealing to hear her talk about sex and about her men. She made no effort to hide the fact that she'd had her share, and planned on having her as many as she could get her hands on.

When conversation lagged, the bottle filled in. When the bottle stopped having meaning, our bodies sought each other out, delighting in the by-ways of sex, of which she was amazingly skilled—far more sophisticated and skilled than years before. The passion she'd offered then had now been honed with a lot of experience. Where she had been highly passionate, now she was amazingly a pure mistress of love-making.

It was late in the morning when we finally got dressed and left the beach house. Linda drove me back to the cocktail lounge at which we'd met, and where I'd left my car. Before parting we exchanged phone numbers and addresses. I gave her my card, and wrote the information she'd given me on the back of another of it. We kissed passionately goodbye and promised each other to make contact soon.

I watched Linda drive off down Wilshire, and then slowly went to my car. I drove home thinking I would have much rather have spent the weekend with her; but she had claimed to have other plans that she couldn't break.

I lay in bed thinking about the next time I'd see Linda, the next time that I'd hold lovely body in my arms, and feel the pleasure of her love-making. She was great. It wasn't hard to think about something serious with Linda. Of course, unlike the kid who

17

had enjoyed her years ago and dreamed fantasy illusions, I was mature enough to recognized the impossibility of that ever happening with her. She was a free spirit, for one thing, and outclassed me socially for another—not that the latter really mattered to her; it was simply a fact of life.

But we had something going, and I figured on enjoying that for as long as it could last.

I fell asleep with dreams of calling her in the next few days.

If only I'd known what the next day would bring, I might not have let her leave me. What I thankfully didn't know that night was that I'd never see Linda again. Not alive that is.

CHAPTER II.

The ringing of the phone jarred me awake. For a moment I couldn't remember my surroundings. I had the feeling of still being next to Linda; then I remembered leaving her.

Sleepily I climbed out of bed and groped my way toward the phone that was in the living room.

"Hello, who is it, damn it!" I growled.

"Stan Maxton?" a gruff voice inquired.

"Yes, who's this?"

"Lt. Hanson, homicide."

"What's up, now? I haven't gotten any speed tickets I don't know about, have I?"

"Don't be smart. You're wanted down here, right away. We'd have sent a car, but because of your private detective license we thought you'd be willing to cooperate. Some questions about a woman named Linda Harryington. It seems she knew you or she was hiring you for a job. She had your card in her purse."

"What's this all about?" I demanded. The sleep

had suddenly smashed away. I was now fully awake.

"She was found murdered in her beach house, this morning. Her head was bashed in."

For a moment I couldn't quite convince myself that I'd heard right.

Linda dead? It didn't seem possible.

As I stood there, dazed, staggered under the sudden unexpected blow, my mind lived over all the moments we had shared that summer so many years before. A summer ended with a direct announcement from Ralph Harryington that the affair stop. Luckily we'd pretty much run our course in some ways; though didn't fully understand that at the time. He had given Linda tickets to Europe and said to use them.

Pain, both physical and emotional, jarred me. Last night she had been so alive, so wonderful. Then another thought shook me. If they finger-printed the place they'd have me as a number one suspect. And that was another matter, completely. Another danger! They would have a hell of a time connecting a motive; but if they looked far enough, and got a good D.A. on the case, they just might be able to convince a grand jury.

Suddenly I wanted to see Lt. Hanson as much as he wanted to see me.

"Where do I meet you?" I inquired.

"At the Santa Monica Station. Get the hell down here right away or we'll have an all out dragnet looking for you," he informed me in a rough voice.

"Don't push, buddy. I'll be there." Without another word I hung up and then started dressing.

The drive to Santa Monica took over an hour;

Saturday traffic to the beach was highly congested. Each moment was an agony of remembering Linda; feeling the personal loss.

When I arrived at the Police Station, I was ushered into one of those drab offices in which detectives make it a habit of questioning witnesses and suspects. The officer-escort told me to wait there.

Lighting a cigarette, I sat down in one of those uncomfortable wood chairs, which look more like something from an outdated school for children. I tried to calm my nerves and hold down the grind at the pit of my stomach. I tried to be unemotional.

Even if you don't have an emotional attachment for a broad, it's quite a jolt to discover that the one you've just shacked up with the night before has been killed. Somebody like Linda made it even more tragic. She was too beautiful to be killed at such a young age. And it was one hell of a lot more than just a casual thing I'd felt toward her.

The cigarette was down to a butt when the door opened and a huge framed man stepped in. He introduced himself as Lt. Hanson.

I lighted another cigarette and waited for the other man to make his play. I'd learned years ago that the only way to play safe was to listen, then counter the verbal attack. If attack fight and ask questions later. What ever they knew, or thought they knew, had to be limited; I wasn't about to give them more information than necessary.

"How long have you known Linda Harryington?" Hanson demanded in a dipped tone of voice; each word was chopped off, accented.

"Last night. I picked her up at the bar and then—"

"Oh, come on, Mr. Maxton. You don't expect me to believe a story like that, do you?"

I beamed like an innocent child. "It's the truth. Believe what you want."

"Don't play games with me! Miss Harryington comes from a very rich family. She was a good looking woman—she didn't have to go around picking men up. Besides that she was engaged to Philip Baxtar, II. Now, do you want to go over the story from the beginning?"

I was mentally staggered over the information that had been rammed into my gut. I'd known she had money of course; but I didn't have any knowledge of how much. If she was connected with Phil Baxtar, her family had to have plenty of spending money. Baxtar was beyond the millionaire bracket; he was one of those few people who could buy himself out of publicity. There are very few incredibly rich people in the world; and those few, nobody knew about, unless you were connected in the right circles. Their faces were unknown to the newspapers and the general public.

Suddenly everything was taking on a new turn; a new danger point.

If Phil Baxtar was involved there was a damned good chance that my life was cooked. Once they discovered my prints all over the beach house, they'd lock me up and throw the key away. Baxtar could buy and sell out all of Los Angeles, land, people, dogs, and not even realize he'd spent a dime. That was how rich Baxtar was.

"Where do you want me to start?" I asked, needing the extra moment to consider what I could tell the man. The truth might not be believable; on the

22

other hand, there wasn't any way of getting out of admitting having been at the beach house. They'd discover that fact in short time.

"From the beginning."

I decided to jazz up the facts a little. Maybe the truth wouldn't be believable to anybody except Linda and myself. But Linda was dead.

"I knew her casually, but...well, I didn't want anybody to know about it. We happened to bump into each other last night, and she invited me to the beach house. We had a couple of cocktails and then I left about...ten, I guess. All fully respectable and casual."

"How casually did you know her?" Hanson pushed.

"Oh, we met a long time ago. In Florida, believe."

"Don't you know?"

"I can't remember. We just happened to meet— oh, yes, I believe it was at some party. I'm not sure. Some party given by a client of mine."

"Who?"

"Private information. You know I can't reveal the names of clients. Especially one who has as much money as this one had."

It was a pretty lie, but already I could see where it was going to involve me into a neat web that might trap me up in a death house. With the Baxtar money, Philip II could manage anything he damned pleased. Even the death of a woman like Linda— and get away with it; if somebody didn't nail the evidence on him with an unmovable tack.

I asked: "Does Baxtar know about "

"No. We haven't been able to get hold of him. A

man like Baxtar can disappear pretty easily for months, and then return—we're trying to get hold of him right now. Ralph Harryington, Linda's father, is on his way from New York. Only member of the family was Ann Harryington—a real dish of a woman, must be twenty years younger than Ralph." A gleam showed in the man's eyes.

"Look, you don't think I had anything to do with this, do you?" I inquired, realizing there wasn't any reason to play coy.

Hanson stared at me for a long time and then shook his head. "I don't think so."

"Hell, you can check me out with Chief Turner, he'll—"

"Already have. He came through with a good recommendation. Said you boozed it a little too much, and had a way with the women, but that you're honest. I just wanted to check things out."

"And see where the crumbs fell?" I countered, standing, as if to leave.

"Don't start running out of town. You might be on the suspect list, yet. We can't do much until a little more investigation has gone through the machinery."

I didn't wait to say goodbye. Suddenly all I wanted to do was get good and drunk and forget about Linda Harryington. If that was possible.

I drove directly to my apartment. Once inside I took a bottle of whiskey from the kitchen cupboard and poured myself several ounces in a water glass. I was working on the last few drops of the whiskey when the front door bell rang.

For a moment I thought of ignoring It. Then as the ringing continued, I went to the door and opened it.

"Yes?"

Two expensive three hundred dollar gray-blue suits were standing there. At first I only noticed the suits, not the faces. Then I saw the faces. The tallest man, who was standing closest to me, wore a toothy grin, but his eyes were cold ice. He had the look of soft living and easy life that is seen in employees of rich men. After several years of having worked for rich clients, I'd learned to tell a lot about the way a man dressed and the way they looked at another person. The second man looked hard. He was stocky and had a stupid face.

The soft one said: "My name's Gordon Chambers. You are Stan Maxton?"

"Yes?"

"Well, I represent Mrs. Harryington. Ah, could I come in, please?" He was already stepping into the room and his partner was closing the door behind them.

"By all means, make yourself at home."

"Thank you." Chambers walked to the sofa and sat down. His partner stood by the door; a steel barrier against escape.

I turned and looked at Chambers. "Well, what do I owe this visit to?"

Chambers came right to the point, very businesslike, very brash. "You were the last one to see Linda alive—unless we consider the killer."

I nodded, waiting.

"Could you tell me something about your relationship with her?" Chambers asked.

I started to tell him the same story I'd told Lt. Hanson. He listened politely, and when I finished he said: "Oh, come on, Mr. Maxton. If I got you into court I could cut you to ribbons on that. One thing: Miss Harryington has never been in Florida. And for a second thing: She never knew you before last night!" His smile was friendly, but his eyes hard, narrowed.

For a moment I didn't know if I should be relieved or not. Then I said: "That's the story that Lt. Hanson accepted."

"Oh, we don't have to play games among the three of us. We knew Linda, and we know what kind of life she led. As for the police—let them believe that version. Do you want to tell me what really happened?"

I studied Chambers for a long time and then said: "Well, I picked her up at a cocktail lounge in Beverly Hills. She had me drive her car to the beach house, where we had cocktails and made love."

The man smiled nastily: "Love? Really!"

"Okay Call it sex if you want. Later, about three or four, we returned to Beverly Hills where my car was parked. I gave her my card, and she gave me her phone and address. Then she drove off in the direction of L.A. That's the last I saw of her. It's the truth—but if you don't want to believe that your little darling didn't do exactly that, then—"

"I believe you. It follows close to pattern. She did this all the time." Chambers hesitated; then said: "You're a private detective?"

I nodded.

"A good one, so I'm told from the short investigation we've been able to make on you in a little less than thirty minutes. You'll have to forgive me if I've been a little round-about in getting to the actual

26

business that we have in mind. Mrs. Harryington has instructed me to hire you to find Linda's killer. I understand that you charge five thousand for such a case, plus expenses."

"You're well informed," I snapped, acidly.

"That's what I'm paid for." He stood and stepped towards me, extending his hand. "You'll take the case."

It wasn't a question; more a command.

I looked at him, annoyed. I didn't like the set-up; I didn't like the goon who was standing at my door; and I didn't like Chambers or his methods. Then I thought about Linda; and I thought about what a man like Baxtar could do to me if he decided I was the most likely suspect.

"Okay. So I'll play along. What now?" I ignored the other's hand that slowly fell to his side.

"You'll come with us. Mrs. Harryington wants to see you, first. She'll be able to give you information about Linda that should help to start you in the right direction."

Without another word I followed the man out of my apartment.

We were driven through town in a large, black, custom made Lincoln. It was a little over twenty minutes drive to the Harryington Beverly Hills home. The house was a cozy little two story rambling place that must have had no more than thirty rooms, and cost no more than a couple of billion dollars. Well, maybe that was somewhat on the high side, but even then I couldn't have afforded it even in a dream. I'd seen rich homes before, but this one took the prize.

We went up to the door, Chambers rang, a maid

answered, let us in and led us to a small living room that was a one plus advertisement for European hand-carved furnisher. There I was to wait for the arrival of Mrs. Harryington. The lawyer withdrew, saying he'd be ready to take me back when I was finished.

I had time to think about the events that had so quickly closed in on me. First the night with Linda and her sex-starved body; then being informed of her death, and the fear that the police might try to pin it on me; then finding out about Phil Baxtar II being engaged to Linda; and now this sudden turn.

I wondered what Mrs. Harryington would be like. A matron, high classed and a little high nosed; cold and distant. She was Linda's step-mother, and much younger than her husband.

Then the double doors, which led into some other room beyond, opened and a lovely young woman in her late twenties or early thirties, stepped into the room.

I looked, wondering if this might be Linda's sister. The woman was dressed in a blue sheath that revealed enough of her curves to cause quite human reactions to race through my body. Her breasts were high and well formed; the flesh, which showed where the neckline dipped, was white and creamy looking. She had long, delicate fingers, and red painted nails. She stood there, regal and distant; but fully aware of her womanly attractiveness. A silver streak, which was obviously unnatural, whipped through the front of her raven black hair.

"Are you Mr. Maxton?" she inquired in a cultured, but husky voice.

"Yes," I managed, finding it hard to keep my

eyes from running over her delightfully stacked figure. She was the kind of woman that any man would like to have as a secretary, which I automatically assumed her to be.

"I'm Mrs. Harryington. Would you come into my office?" she inquired.

I stared, stunned. For a moment it wasn't possible to conceal my shock. Then I slowly nodded and followed her into the other room.

CHAPTER III.

The room was bookcase-lined; it looked more like a study than an office. I didn't have time to give it a very complete examination before Mrs. Harryington demanded my full attention. "What do you know of Linda?"

"Nothing much," I admitted. Suddenly I was aware of the awkwardness of the situation. She wanted to know what had happened between me and her step-daughter; it wasn't easy to consider telling the family about intimacies with one of their members.

"You slept with Linda?" Her voice was matter of fact. She looked at me as she lighted a cigarette.

I shrugged. "We met at a bar last night."

"I thought that might be it." Her eyes lowered and then she looked at the far wall. "Linda wasn't the kind of woman that played around at life—she lived it, fully."

She was thoughtful for a moment and then continued, this time looking directly at me. "Maybe I should tell you something about myself, Linda, and the family situation."

She motioned to a tan leather sofa. "Would you like a drink?"

Suddenly that sounded like a good idea.

I nodded. She went to the desk, which was perched in the middle of the room. In moments she had pulled out a bottle of Scotch from a drawer, and two glasses. "No ice."

"That's fine. Doesn't matter." My eyes were playing along the curving lines of Mrs. Harrying-ton's body. She couldn't be over thirty-two; possibly only twenty-eight. It was hard to tell her actual age because of the way she carried herself; the way her face was made up to look more mature and re-gal. I had the feeling that she purposely was at-tempting to bridge the gap between her own age and that of her husband. She leaned over while pouring the drinks and I had a full view of her large well-shaped breasts. She happened to look up for a mo-ment, and her eyes met mine. Just the suggestion of a smile moved the corners of her full lips upward. It could have been amusement, or something else.

As she walked across the room I noticed the un-conscious jerk of her hips. I was sure it wasn't an action that was put on for affect, but rather a natural habit of hers.

I took the drink she offered, and she sat down beside me.

"I guess," she began, after sipping her Scotch, "you think this is quite a weird set-up. A step-daughter hardly younger than the 'mother'.... Maybe if I explained that Linda and myself were friends in college that would clear things up a bit. We ran around in the same crowd even if I was a senior when she was a Freshman. In any case, I was invited to a party here at the house, and Ralph seemed to take a liking to me. His wife had been dead for a couple of years, and he was lonely. In any case the romance was pretty rapid. When it was over, I was Mrs. Harryington."

"Then you must have been pretty close to Linda," I suggested.

"Close enough to do a lot of things together. It seems as if we did more things together than Ralph and myself. But that's more because my husband is pretty busy." She took another swallow of her drink and then suddenly changed the subject. "What I want you to do is to find who killed Linda—if that's possible. I think you'll know what to do then."

I nodded. "Do you have any ideas? Who might have killed her?"

"There might have been many. A jealous lover. Who knows?" She shrugged, the action moved her breasts in a very sensually intriguing way.

"What about this Phil Baxtar? I understand he was engaged to Linda."

Mrs. Harryington laughed, then said: "Phil couldn't care less—if that's what you're trying to say! He isn't the jealous type. Sure he knew about her little escapades. But that wasn't important to him. He wanted to marry her—it was a complicated situation. Linda is beautiful and—well she was, oh, it's hard to get used to...the way..." She broke off and covered her face in her hands.

"Mrs. Harryington, I..." My arm went around her shoulder. For a moment I was startled by the sensual feel of her. She was a strikingly attractive woman.

After a moment she gained control over her

emotions and gently moved away. " I'm sorry."

"That's all right, Mrs. Harry—"

"No. Call me Ann. None of this formal stuff. I always feel stiff and stuffy when people call me Mrs. Harryington. After all, I'm not that much of a matron. Not yet. And hopefully *never*!"

"You're a very attractive young woman...Ann."

"Thank you." She sat there for a moment longer and then returned the conversation to Linda and Baxtar. "Phil wanted to marry Linda because she would make a good wife—and good hostess. A well-bred woman to have around the house. If she played her little parlor games—that didn't make any difference to him. He had his women, too."

"Isn't that a little weird?" I managed, surprised by her statement.

"Not at all. Phil has the money to keep any escapades out of the paper. In any case, nobody in the public is interested in Phil Baxtar—because nobody knows who he is. That's what happens when you are that rich. Ralph can do a lot of that 'buying silence" too, but not as completely as Phil. You have to understand that when a man has as much money as Phil has, he can buy and sell anybody in the country. You realize that Phil—if he were to cash in on his holdings—is worth many billions of dollars?"

"I've heard something about him. And about how he hates publicity. I've heard about him, but never seen his picture."

"See what I mean?" She finished off her Scotch and then continued. "In any case, Phil wants a family, and he picked Linda because she had the looks and the background and the knowledge of handling wealth. And the fact that they knew each other since childhood. It was arranged many years ago by Ralph and Phil Baxtar I."

"I didn't know that still went on."

"It does, more than you know. In a rather subtle way, mind you. But just the same. Family matching family. Status marrying into status. Business deals, sometimes. In any case, Linda and Phil had made quite a realistic arrangement between themselves. In time, they would marry and in time they would settle down and have a family. And possibly while they were married they would have their lovers— that was something both had felt should be worked out when the time came around. In any case, they had agreed to have their fling while they could. Next year they were supposed to get married. It's all very simple, if you understand the background and the complexities involved. They're intelligent— well, Linda was and Phil is, intelligent in his way and very modern in his outlook on life. Plus, at this level, socially, quite, well-managed affairs can be the norm."

"But all you've managed to do is tell me why Phil Baxtar is out of the picture as a possible jealous lover killer. Where does that leave me?"

"I can give you a list of people to see, who might lead you onto something. And I'll give you the police report, when we get it, and the key to the beach house, in case you want to look around. But I can point out one thing that might help you. Linda had a lot of men whom she played around with, socially, who wanted to marry her, and there were the others, like yourself, whom, she merely picked up. I can have my secretary typing up a list of Linda's personal friends, and, some of the men she picked up, and the places where she hung out. From that you should be able to get a fairly good start."

"Like finding a needle in that famous haystack."

"But it should be something to get you on the right stack of hay."

"If you could only give me the name of the killer, I'd be a lot more happy, "I announced dryly.

Ann Harryington laughed delightedly. "You are quite a kidder, aren't you, Mr. Maxton?"

"Stan," I offered.

She smiled. It was the kind of intimate, secret expression which is both suggestive and distant. "Stan it is, then, Stan."

She stared at me for a moment and then impulsively reached out a hand for mine. The contact was electric. For a moment I had the almost overwhelming urge to pull her into my arms, and kiss her lush lips.

For some reason I felt that would be accepted by her in a very casual, pleased manner.

I had the uneasy feeling that the loose freedom of having lovers wasn't confined to Linda and Phil Baxtar. Ann Harryington looked like the kind of woman that climbed into bed with any likely man, as a kind of pleasant exercise, just for the hell of it. Some people jogged, others took lovers.

The fact that she was a client and married had nothing to do with my holding back the desire; it was something else, which I couldn't quite understand at the moment. Instinct over-powered automatic desire.

Maybe it was the conviction that she would be more than willing to be kissed, and a lot more. The idea of becoming more involved with the Harryington family than I already was, seemed a bit fool-hardy.

The moment passed and her hand slipped silently away.

She stood and looked down at me. For a moment she seemed at a loss as to what to say. Then finally, awkwardly, in a much too husky voice, said: "Well, I'll go see if Emma has the information ready yet."

She was just reaching for the door, opposite the double entrance in which I'd entered the room, when there was a timid knock on it. She opened the door and a tall, middle-aged woman stood there.

"The papers," the newcomer announced, handing Ann Harryington an envelope.

Ann thanked the woman and then closed the door, stepping across the room to me.

"This should give you all the Information you need to start your investigation. There's a check enclosed for five hundred, for expenses. If you need more of anything, just ring." She smiled quite pleasantly and extended her hand for him. "It was a pleasure meeting you, Stan. I hope we'll see each other again, soon—under more enjoyable circumstances."

The soft huskiness in her voice seemed to imply more than a casual conversation; but I decided that was merely my imagination running over-time to meet the racing riot of my racing pulse.

Ann Harryington was a sensually beautiful package to tempt a man to unwrap her.

As I left the Harryington home, escorted by Gordon Chambers, I found my thoughts racing over the possibilities of what it might be like to discover how far Ann Harryington would really go if a man—me, in this instance—were to make a pass at her.

The drive back to my apartment was a stony silence. I merely said goodbye to Chambers and went into my apartment.

Once the door had been closed behind me, I opened the envelope.

There was a list of names and addresses:

Sherry Anderson.
Bill Carver.
Henry Davis
Jay Eaton.
Mary Jenkins.
Charlie Manners
Dora Norton.
Ned Peters.
Frank Peters.
Walter Stevens.
Larry Turner.
Sam Winters.

Three women and nine men. The addresses were scattered all over Los Angeles County. Under each name was the relationship between them and Linda. All the men were either casual "pick-up" lovers, or long range male friends. The women were social friends. No comments were made as to their importance or further connection with Linda. It was going to be like playing a quiz game to see how much information I might be getting, before the police decided that I could easily be a number one suspect and make out a warrant for my arrest; which I was sure they'd get around to, sooner or later, if some-body better didn't come into the picture.

A man in my business gets to know something about the workings of rich people, especially—and the police force. When the police are under pressure of rich money or politics, they can make some pretty hasty selections, in order to calm the families involved. Not that they'll railroad a guy into the hot chair, but they'll make things pretty "hot" for them, until the real villain is caught. I had no plans of be-ing made a goat in this set-up. And I had the uneasy feeling that with Phil Baxtar in the picture, things would get pretty hot for me. Any man, no matter how "modern" he might be with his loved one, will make a pretty big show when it comes to the death of his fiancé. I was the last known person to see Linda; therefore, I was the logical one to pick on.

There was a list of half a dozen night clubs in which Linda was known to hang. With the names of friends and the clubs, I had a long, long work-out ahead of me.

I fixed myself a couple of shots of whiskey. Un-dressed, showered and got into a new suit of clothes. Checked the .38 snub-nose revolver as I strapped its holster around my chest, and then poured myself another strong drink.

The life of a detective doing foot work is a tiring and boring business; I wasn't looking forward to the next hours, and possibly days of investigation. Maybe if I'd known about the three women on my list, I might have been a little more interested in the coming events. But I couldn't know that, then. It wasn't until coming face to face with this trio of loveliness that I would really begin to appreciate the complexities of this case. Some delightful; some horrifying.

Making sure that I was well supplied with cash and had the list Ann Harryington had given me, I finished off my whiskey and headed for the door.

I was just opening it when two men shoved me back into my room. Both were tough and rugged-looking.

One pinned me against the wall and the other grabbed my coat collar.

" Stan Maxton?" the man holding my collar inquired.

I made a rasping sound in my throat which must have given him the answer to his question. He nodded and then sank a fist into the pit of my stomach.

My body is steel hard, and it can take a good beating before it finally gives in under the pressure of pain.

But the two men knew their business and in a matter of minutes there were stars bursting in front of my eyes.

The fist kept hammering at my guts, into my face and throat, chest, and finally something slammed up into my groin.

I felt acid begin to erupt up through my throat as blackness started to slowly sink me into a deep dark pool that hungrily devoured all consciousness.

CHAPTER IV.

It was like coming out of a long sleep, wading through a thick black fog. For a long time I was only aware of being aware, then slow pain began to ebb through my body. I couldn't remember what had happened last. I tried to think back, but only visions of Linda and visions of her step-mother, the lovely Ann Harryington, raced through my mind.

Slowly the thoughts became clearer and I began to remember other things.

A moan sounded and I wondered who might be there in the room with me; then I realized the moan came from my own lips.

After a moment I tried to move and pain stabbed through me. I opened my eyes and found myself looking up at the ceiling of my living room.

Then I remembered what had happened; the two men and the unexpected beating.

With an angry curse I forced myself into a sitting position. Then slowly my fingers searched over the sore spots, checking to see if any serious damage had been done. After a couple of painful moments I discovered that besides a few possible bruises, I was in fairly good shape.

Standing, I went into the kitchen, poured myself a drink and sat down, trying to decide who had sent the goon squad, and why they had been sent.

The only logical answers I was able to come up with were: Either Baxtar had learned about my little night with Linda, and arranged for a battering job or it was the killer, who wanted to get me out of the picture. Both seemed unreasonable.

Finally, after having finished off my drink, I stood, went to the bathroom, cleaned my face and pulled off my shirt to examine the pain-spots on my chest and stomach. My face had been hammered pretty good, the nose had bled a lot and my lips were swollen.

After showering and changing, I left the apartment. My first destination was one of the clubs mentioned on the list that Ann Harryington had given me.

The next hours were revealing, but gave little information of the kind which I wanted.

"...Oh, sure. I know Linda. She comes in here all the time. Usually picks up some guy and leaves," one bartender claimed.

"Linda Harryington. A sweet kid. Comes in with a date and has a couple of drinks and then leaves with her date," another bartender Informed me.

Slowly a picture began to take painful shape. Linda had presented herself as a different kind of person at each bar. One guy claimed she was a hustler. Another bartender said she never would look at men. Would come in for a drink and turn down all offers. The pattern seemed to be that at some places she acted like the lady she was supposed to be; at other bars, usually dives, she was a bitch in heat, looking over the men and picking out one or another for an exchange of flirtation that would end up with her leaving with the man.

It was late in the morning when I returned to my apartment and fell asleep, exhausted. The only thing I'd learned for my efforts was that Linda had apparently led different lives. I began to believe she might have been nothing more than a rich thrill seeker; living on booze and men and money. If I had never known her, that's the impression I'd get as a PI.

The next morning I examined the list of names that had been given me. Somewhere on the list could be the killer; on the other hand it might turn out to be as useless as the nightclub-bar list.

I decided to take it from the top and work my way down the list.

Sherry Anderson lived in Encino, in the San Fernando Valley. The address indicated an apartment house. I took the Hollywood freeway to the Balboa turn-off in Encino and then went to Havenhurst and Moorpark.

The apartment was middle classed, and I guessed the rent couldn't be more than $255 a month for a one bedroom. I searched out apartment 5, and rang the doorbell.

It was about ten in the morning and when there wasn't an immediate answer I began to doubt that Sherry Anderson was home. Chances were, so I reasoned, that she was out working.

When the door suddenly burst open and a tall, bleached blonde stood there in a house robe, which was tightly pulled around her slender figure, 1 wasn't prepared. For a moment I stood there in a stunned daze.

"Well?" she asked in a high, cheap sounding voice. Her hard blue eyes studied me. "What you want?"

"You Sherry Anderson?"

"So, what's it to you, buddy?" She stood there, one hand on the door, ready to slam it shut. She didn't look afraid, or concerned about a stranger asking for her. She was more annoyed. There was a hardness to her angular features; but they also had a sensual attractiveness. I classified her as an easy pick-up; the kind of girl that will spread her legs for any comers.

"Ann Harryington gave me your name. Said you knew Linda pretty well. And—"

"Oh, god, yes! I heard about what happened to Linda. It was horrible, wasn't it?" She smiled warmly, but didn't make any move to invite me into her apartment.

"I wanted to find out something about Linda. I'm trying to get a line on who might have—"

"Oh, come on in. I'll tell you what I know. Maybe it'll help. I don't know for sure. Come on in." She opened the door wide and closed it after me.

For a long time she stood there, leaning against the door, studying me. Then she said:

"You a private detective?"

"Yeah."

"I thought so. The police look different. A girl gets to know. And I was expecting somebody like you—Ann would hire a private dick."

"Have any idea who might have killed Linda?" I

inquired casually.

She thought for a moment, her lips pursing tightly together. Then she shook her head. "No one in particular. But I can suggest several who might have had motives."

I felt a mixture of excitement and relief. For the first time it looked as if I was going to get at least a shove in the right direction.

I looked at Sherry, and our eyes met. There was a crude expression of excitement in her eyes; I wasn't sure if it were because of myself, or because of what she was going to tell me. But, of course, she had a lot of sex-appeal, just there in her face. She was the kind of woman that I'd known in many sizes and shapes; the type that a man will rack up with for an evening of pleasure and forget all about her after she's out of sight.

"I guess you didn't know Linda, did you?" Sherry inquired, walking cat-like across the room and settling down on the sofa. Her robe parted slightly. I kept my eyes away from her body and tried to keep my attention on her face.

"I knew her for an evening if that's enough," I lied. Sherry's eyebrows raised; interest showed on her face. "Was she as good as everybody says?"

"What?"

"Good in bed?"

"That's none of your business."

She frowned. Then her robe parted slightly. A creamy white breast peeked out through the opening. Sherry didn't make any attempt to hide the nudity of the pert pink point of her breast. She smiled as she saw the direction of my gaze.

"I was just interested. She had quite a reputation. The men went for her—it was hard to be in the same room with her. A girl had to fight with everything she had to keep up with the competition."

"You shouldn't have been worried," I pointed out; this time my eyes ran over the full length of her body, blatantly appraising her like a pimp judging some girl in his string.

"You really think so?" She sounded pleased. For a moment she was silent. "I bet you know how to do a woman real good."

I coughed and tried to keep my mind on the matter of getting information about Linda.

"Tell me something about Linda."

Sherry stared at me for a moment and then shrugged. "Linda liked men. She didn't play the tramp, but she picked up a lot of guys. She thought of it as something to do. and didn't think of it as being a tramp. She liked sex and couldn't get enough...but then there was that engagement. You know she was engaged to Phil Baxtar?"

"Yes, I heard about it. Weren't they in love?"

"Who knows? They didn't act like it when they weren't together. Sometimes I'd see them together and they were quite friendly—I mean well, they were real cozy-like—but...you could never tell about Linda, or Phil for that matter." She hesitated and her eyes looked over my large frame. "I can understand why she picked up with you. You're the type she liked. Rugged. Hard and good-looking. She liked tall men. And she liked real hard ones! But then who doesn't?" Sherry laughed, then added: "I like you, too."

"Thanks, honey, but I'm on a case."

She shrugged again and then continued:

46

"Well, anyway, there were a lot of guys who would hate her enough—or love her enough—to kill her, I guess. And maybe a few girls. She took a lot of men away from a lot of girls. She took Sam Winters away from me. I hated her... for that, for awhile. Then I realized she had probably done me a favor. Hell, if a man looks for another woman, he can't care very much about you, can he?"

"I guess not."

"Anyway, it really doesn't matter. I don't like long attachments. I've come to the point where it is more fun to just play the field, if you know what I mean. Sorta like Mistress of the Ballgame. I get to—"

I laughed at that, cause her hands were palm up, bouncing invisible balls, like a juggler. She smiled warmly at my reaction.

"Well, you get my point, I see!" Her robe had fallen a bit more open. It didn't at all seem to matter to her; in fact it seemed like she'd somehow managed to make it shiver looser about her body.

I nodded, trying to ignore the delightful point of her breast that had already begun to inch further out from the narrow part at her neckline.

"Don't you think you should pull that thing around your body?" I finally inquired in a much more husky voice than I would have wished to have.

Already a heated, normal male desire was beginning to have its natural effects over my mind and body. It was tempting to think about rolling on a bed with Sherry Anderson. Men, including myself, are basically pigs when it comes to reacting to a seductive situation, or an exposed flash of female flesh. We're natural suckers. The situation was enough to spark even the dullest of imaginations. No woman will allow a naked breast to show unless she's pretty willing to show all, and share it. Unless she was an outright nasty tease. I couldn't help being tempted by my natural male thoughts.

"Does it bother you? Me ... letting you see whatever you are seeing?" She looked amazingly innocent, sounded huskily aroused and was being blatantly flirtatious.

"Yes—what do you think?"

She laughed and then opened the top of her robe wider.

"I bet you'd like me better than you did Linda."

"What the hell!"

"Oh, come on, we're adults, now aren't we?" she giggled, delighted by my explosive reaction.

"Damn it!" I cursed, looking away. "Cover yourself."

"Don't you like it? I mean... by body?" she demanded, standing and crossing the room toward me.

"Look, baby, under other circumstances I'd give you a real wild party, if that's what you wanted, but this isn't the time and the place. Just tell me about Linda."

"If I say it's the time and place, would that make a difference?" she challenged, now standing over me, her robe fully parted. Her fists were on her hips. "What's wrong with you? Don't you like a girl who offers herself? I think you're cute—and I don't mind admitting it. Most of the crowd that Linda ran around with liked sex—we didn't try to hide it. So...what's the beef? Or don't you have any?"

Her eyes went to my groin like a moth to a flame, then popped up to meet mine. "I think you

48

have the beef!"

She explosively laughed, almost giggling in delight at her statement, and that caused her breasts to jiggle widely, attracting my eyes.

I swallowed hard, finding it overwhelmingly unbelievable that a woman could play such a brazen game with a strange man. "Look, we don't even know each other."

"You didn't know Linda, did you? Picked her up?"

"That's none of your..."

"My business? Hell, what's wrong with a little hard ball? Aren't you a sportin' man? I like it. Enjoy playing bat or catcher—any position is just dandy to me, and I'll go first, second, third or home plate. In fact I'm a plate full of goodies, creamy and hot and able to smear myself all over you. And to be honest, honey, I'd like to do just that to you!"

"Later, sometime, okay?" I smiled.

She stared at me, a little surprised, then amused. "Most guys I know wouldn't turn down an offer like that. But...You're okay, I guess."

After a moment she slowly pulled the robe around her body. "I'm a stripper, you know. You'll have to come down and see me, sometime." She shrugged and then walked back to the sofa.

I was sweating and my hands were already beginning to shake. It seemed incredible that a woman could be so bold in front of a stranger. Not that I hadn't had my share of hot pickups from time to time. But this was totally different.

There was a long silence and then I finally asked: "Mind starting all over, honey?"

"With the sex bit?" Her face brightened. "You

ready for a real strip? I'm very good, you can imagine. And my private show is something wild. I promise you."

"Hell, no. Some other time. Business before pleasure. About Linda."

She sighed, both disappointed and somewhat philosophical about it. "Well, there was Walt and Charlie, both of them had it real hard on her…and they wanted to marry Linda. And there was Dora—Dora Norton—she wanted real love and was having a swinging time with Walt when Linda walked in on them and took over. End of romance. You might look into their movements…and—"

"And what about you. What were you doing the night before last?" I jabbed out at her.

She laughed. "In bed with a friend. You can check that out. I guess you've been given Henry Davis" name, he'll tell you."

"What kind of crowd did Linda run around with? I mean, well…"

"We're a modern group. Some of us are in show business, others are merely rich by the efforts of their fathers We lived it up, believe in having a ball while you can—does that explain what you wanted to know?"

"Anything else you can tell me that might be interesting?"

"You kidding? How long you want to stay? Linda balled it with anything with pants on. She was super charged for love and men and hot sex."

I stood and thanked Sherry, starting for the door. She rushed ahead of me, getting there first. Her robe was completely open and I had a full view of every lovely curve of her slender form.

50

"Look, baby, I could use it. Believe me. All this talk has got me hot. Very hot. And you're great looking. You'd do me a favor." She slid her arms around my neck and before it was possible to do anything to stop her, her lips crushed to mine. The softness of her breasts pressed against my chest. I felt the probing dart of her moist tongue as it attempted to press into my mouth.

Shock, mixed with my already stimulated desires, overwhelmed resistance.

Suddenly 1 didn't care about anything. It didn't matter that she was a little bitch in heat, and that we didn't even know each other. Her body was trembling against mine, her tongue deep in my mouth, hungrily searching.

I crushed her against me and as our lips parted, she moaned in delight.

"I knew you'd like it. I bet you'll like it better with me—I know you'll like me better than Linda." She rotated her hips against mine. "I'm really hot and much better! Believe me! I know things from my stripping experience that'll drive you wild!"

Sanity returned.

"Look, honey, let's not go crazy—this just isn't the time for such "

Her hand reached for me in a most suggestive way and all at once the wildness to possess her was in complete control. Or, rather, let her possess what she was already fondling.

"You bitch!" I cursed, yanking her in my arms. We kissed there for a long time and then she pulled away and led me toward the bedroom.

Just then, as it seldom does in real life, the door bell rang. Sherry quickly arranged her robe around her body and answered it.

CHAPTER V.

Under the circumstances, considering the intimacy that had been promised, almost against my will, it was maddening, while at the same time a relief to have the interruption. It would give me time to think matters out. Sherry Anderson opened the door and then jerked back.

"Cops!" she moaned. "What the hell do you want?"

The voice of Lt. Hanson soothed through the apartment. "Well, well, look what we found. You're really in this thicket, sonny boy!"

The man's eyes were darting my way like spears.

"Just doing a little private investigating," I pointed out with a crooked, innocent smile.

"Well, take your fancy PI behind and get out of here!"

"Hey, you are breaking up a private party!" I objected. The choice of leaving Sherry with this guy or balling it with her, now made the invitation of her hungry arms all the more inviting.

Lt. Hanson grinned as his eyes stripped over

Sherry's robe covered body. The woman looked pleased as she returned the gaze. It was almost as if Sherry had already shifted her interest to other man.

"Well, easy come, easy go!" I sighed, walking past the Lieutenant.

Sherry glanced at me, her expression was pleading. "You don't have to leave, hon."

"Sorry, baby, when the law says jump—that's what I do! Hippy hop!" I left the apartment as fast as my legs would carry me before the Lieutenant got ideas about giving me the third degree. I couldn't help thinking he wouldn't get too much information from Sherry Anderson. I almost wished I could be a fly to observe his reaction to her routine, assuming she pulled it on the cop.

Back behind the wheel of my car, I headed for the freeway and Hollywood, already having mentally noted the second name on the list.

Bill Carver didn't sound as interesting as Sherry had been, but more of a solid, sane person to question than the sex starved, wacky stripper.

I didn't know Bill Carver! And was he a surprise.

As I drove along the Hollywood freeway, my thoughts kept returning to the hot offer of Sherry's body. Finally I turned off at the Highland ramp and headed for Yucca Street. In moments I found the address I was seeking. It was a small, modern apartment that catered to, according to their sign, singles only. I searched for apartment 7 and then walked up the steps. Knocking on the door, I waited.

After a moment the door opened and a man with a two day beard shoved his face out at me.

"What you want? I'm not buying!" The door almost slammed in my face, but I pushed my foot in the right, direction at the right time.

"Questions about Linda Harryington!" I offered. "More interested?"

"What about her?" His eyes narrowed, his thin lips compressed into thinner lines.

"Read the papers?"

"Don't have the time!"

"Watch television?"

"What's that?"

"Linda's dead!" I threw at him.

He stared at me for a moment and then opened the door. I walked into the small, one room apartment, took the place in with one sweep of my eyes.

It was a mess. The sofa had blankets thrown all over it, the coffee table was a mass of ashtrays filled to the brim with cigarette butts. To one side, against the wall, was one of those desks that furnished apartments throw in for kicks, cheap and light, so-called modern. There was a pile of papers on the desk, next to an old portable typewriter.

I turned, looking at the man.

He was standing against the closed door, his face bone white, eyes distant.

"I can't believe it!" Bill Carver finally said, shaking his head. "I need a drink!"

He opened a drawer in the desk and pulled out a bottle of gin. Opening the bottle, Bill Carver gulped, then recapped the bottle, replacing it in the drawer. He turned, looking at me.

"Who are you?"

"I'm asking the questions."

"What do you want?"

"Where were you the night before last, in the morning?"

He frowned. "In bed, where everybody is."

"Before?"

"At the typewriter. I'm a writer or, rather, attempting to write. Sold a few things...Linda had helped a little in introducing me to some editors in the past. I..." His voice choked and then he sat down at the desk chair, staring at his hands. "I can't believe she's...dead. How'd it happen?"

"Somebody decided to cheat nature."

His bloodshot eyes popped up to mine.

"Murdered?" He said the word like it was some vile thing that made him sick.

I merely nodded. "Want to tell me something about her?"

"What do you want...to know?" He straightened and looked at me evenly.

"Everything you know!"

He shrugged. "Not too much. I met her at a bar...and we came up here for a party. She stayed the night and through the next day. I read her some of my things and she thought they were good, said she'd call up a man she knew who might be able to help me."

"She did?"

"Right then. An editor for one of the men's adventure magazines. He made an appointment to see me."

"Who is he?"

"Ned Peters. A youngish guy, but knows his stuff. His father is an agent-writer and now publisher with Ned. They work together. Ned does the editing, Frank over-sees and carries on his agenting

56

and..."

"How well did Linda know them?"

He shrugged. "I guess she bedded with Ned. But she never said, if that's what you mean."

"When did you see her last?"

"Well over a month ago. She came by for a lark. And made like a lovely, beautiful bird, fluttering her wings all around me. Wanted to see how her 'writer" was getting along. We spent the night together, and she went home the next morning."

"How many times did you see her?"

"Half a dozen or so."

I felt a mental stab. It seemed incredible that the woman whom I had fallen in love with some years before could have turned out to be such a wild, easy flyer. Not that I hadn't done a lot of flying, but that's different. The more I got into the case, the stranger it became.

Suddenly I wished I'd never heard bumped into her the other evening. Illusions are sometimes brighter than reality.

"What do you know about her other...men, or Linda?"

"Nothing, really. I picked her up ... she helped me in writing, and then stopped around several times. Check with Ned Peters. She had a lot of pull with him, maybe he knows more than I do."

I studied the man for a few moments and then decided there wasn't much more he could tell me, at least right now.

"Thanks," I said, standing and moving toward the door.

A couple of minutes later I was sitting in my car, looking over the list of names. I decided to jump and go see the Peters" duo. Their office was on Sunset Boulevard, not far from where I was then.

Ten minutes later I was standing in the hallway of a plush office building, looking at a door that was labeled:

NATIONAL PUBLISHERS,
PETRON PUBLISHERS,
FRANK PETERS.

It was impressive.

I walked in and found myself staring into the face of one hell of an attractive woman.

She had flaming red hair and full, lush lips that smiled as she looked up at me.

"Is there anything I can do for you?" she offered in a low, cultured voice. It was the kind of voice you wanted to go to bed with. She was tall, her thrusting breasts, which pushed against the orange blouse, were enough to prove to me that the body that went with the voice was just as inviting.

Everywhere I turned since meeting Linda seemed to offer up lushly shaped women.

Her eyes were deep green and showed only mild interest as they met mine.

"I want to see Ned and Frank Peters."

"What is your business with them?"

"Private."

"Name?"

"Stan Maxton. "

There was only a flicker in her eyes, but it was enough. "I'll see if he's in."

"Come on, just tell him I'm waiting."

She stood, smiled and then wiggled herself

58

across the small office, opened a door and then closed it behind her.

I heard voices and then the door opened again and she smiled out. "Ned will see you, now."

"Thanks!" I said dryly.

Stepping into the inner room I found myself facing a drawing table, desk and a wall of pictures featuring naked women.

So, I thought, one of the famous girlie publishers. Interest shot upwards several degrees.

The receptionist left.

The man sitting behind the desk was broad-shouldered and thick-chested. His eyes were dark, deep-set, almost brooding. He sat there, eyeing me like a hawk. His features were handsome enough, and topped with wavy black hair.

"What can I do for you?" he finally demanded in a low, rasping voice.

"Tell me what you know about Linda Harryington!" I said, coming directly to the point.

His expression didn't change. He merely leaned on his elbows and peered at me. "I knew her socially. She did a couple of pictures for us, under an assumed name and with a wig on. With makeup, even her father couldn't recognize her. Linda got a kick out of posing in the nude."

"That figures," 1 snapped, deciding I didn't like the man. Maybe it was mere jealousy. I was beginning to hate every guy who had laid a finger on Linda.

"What figures?" Ned Peters inquired, his eyes narrowing.

"Linda getting kicks out of posing nude. She seemed to be quite a swinging gal."

"You don't have a right to say that!" he snapped, standing. His features contorted with sudden rage. "Linda was a sweet young girl."

"Oh, come on, don't hand me that!"

"Damn it. Don't you dare come in my office and shit on her name and reputation. I won't have it. Do you hear me?"

"Christ. Calm down! I'm not putting her down."

"Oh, sure. You're trying to tell me she was some kind of slut. I won't have that!" Disgust twisted his features and he leaned across the desk, resting his weight on his extended arms which were balanced against the desk.

"Come on, man. You yourself said she liked displaying her body for the camera and having the pictures plastered all over your magazines. That she enjoyed that thrill—"

"Look, just because a girl gets some kind of kick showing off her body in a respectable magazine...that doesn't mean she's a tramp!" Each word was accented and harsh, grating.

"Linda had a whole line of lovers!" I stated, determined to knife through his defenses.

A surprise came.

Ned Peters slammed back into his swivel chair, his face drew tight. "I don't believe it! And don't you."

"Oh, come on! Surely you knew about her reputation. It was like the newspapers, out there for everybody to read."

"Hell it was!" Ned sounded sick. "I never guessed. I knew her through...well, my dad and her father were old friends. I knew Linda socially. Nothing really happened to indicate that...that she, I just can't believe it."

I stood there, finding it hard to believe that this man, who was obviously aware of the ways of the world and women, could possible have been fooled by Linda. Surely he was either putting me on, or Linda was a pretty clever girl. Rather, had been!

"Okay, tell it from the beginning," I suggested.

"What business it is of yours?" Ned Peters demanded.

"The family hired me to look into the case. That's my business."

"A private eye?"

"Investigator!" I corrected.

"All the same." He took a pack of cigarettes from his shirt pocket, lighted one and then looked up at me. "Like I said, I knew her for a long time. When we were younger we went out together but nothing happened of an intimate nature, even though I tried. After the first turndown, we were good friends. I never tried anything after that. I guess she took me for a chump!"

"Or a good friend?" I offered, sarcastically.

"So, we were good friends."

"What about her?"

"Nothing much. There was a guy, some years back that really shook her up. I know that much. She went to Europe after that. Daddy Harryington commanded and she had to jump."

I felt a sudden wave of excitement shoot through me. "Who was the guy?"

"I don't know. She never mentioned his name. I picked up bits and pieces. He'd been out of the army a short time, she met him at Lake Arrowhead, apparently they had an affair, got serious and her father stepped in for the kill!"

I suddenly wanted to get drunk, run, hide, and never get up again. "Did you see any change in her after that?"

Ned shrugged. "Only that she seemed a little more polished after her trip. That's all. We didn't run around together much during those years. It wasn't until last year that we saw much of each other. She'd come up and...well, talk. She got interested in the magazine and asked about posing for one of them. I tried to talk her out of it, but she was determined. She had a lovely body. She wouldn't pose for anybody but Jay Eaton. He's a friend of hers...maybe they were having an affair, Christ I didn't think about that...I guess she was having one with him, if what you say is true. Actually she did a trick on me. She and Eaton did the pics and Eaton came in with them, said he'd found a new model and thought we would be interested in the spread. Not until after they were published did Linda tell me about it being her. She'd really fixed herself up differently. She had a magnificent body!"

"I know all about her!" I said, then regretted having said it.

"That well?" Ned suggested.

"I didn't say that," I answered back, then asked: "Anything else that might be of interest?"

Ned thought for a moment and then was just about to shrug when he said: "Only that...maybe. It's not important...but she had me help a writer, Bill Carver. I guess she knew him, too." The implication of his last words seemed to hurt. He blinked and then made the shrug of his broad shoulders. "I guess there's a lot I didn't know about Linda..."

I thanked him and then left the office, echoing his last words in my own mind. Every person I talked to about Linda seemed to teach me something new. I didn't know if I should be depressed or over-joyed to discover that I had apparently meant so much to Linda. Now, at least, I'd met one guy who hadn't shacked up with her; that was something, anyway. As I sat in the car, smoking a cigarette, I suddenly realized that I wasn't any closer to discov-ering who had killed Linda than I'd been in the be-ginning. But I was getting a pretty good picture of what kind of life she had led.

Looking at my watch, I realized it was a little past two and I hadn't eaten anything all day. An hour later, a steak digesting with a martini in my stomach, I headed toward Jay Eaton's apartment.

It was a little past three-thirty when I was ring-ing the doorbell of a crummy apartment in the east end of Los Angeles.

The door opened and I looked into the features of a young blonde-haired man, stripped to the waist.

"What the hell do you want?"

"Jay Eaton?"

"Yeah. Well, I'm busy!"

"I want to talk about Linda Harryington."

"Go away!" he snapped nastily, starting to close the door.

I pushed forward, into the apartment.

The living room was a mass of lights and cables. A camera was at one side, a couple feet from the far wall. In the middle of the room was a striking bleached blonde haired woman who immediately snatched my attention. She was naked, posed in a most provocative position.

63

The Sex Cult Murders, by Charles Nuetzel

It was Sherry Anderson.

CHAPTER VI.

"So, we meet again, hon!" Sherry greeted me with a smile, slowly coming to her feet and stretching. Every moment was graceful and sensual. Her breasts rose high on her chest, becoming rounded, firm cones of flesh, calling invitingly.

"What the damned hell are you doing?" Jay Eaton cried, at both of us. "You weren't supposed to move, and you, mister, get the hell out of here!"

Sherry spat out at Eaton: "Don't tell me what to do!"

Eaton took a threatening step toward Sherry. "You do like I say, bitch!"

The two glared dangerously at one another. Then finally Sherry smiled and shrugged. Her large, supple breasts bounced.

This I had to walk out on! I thought. Every muscle tensed at the thought of spending a wild hour in bed with this voluptuous woman.

Eaton twisted around and faced me. "You get out of here or I'll call the police!"

"Calm down, kiddo!" I snapped, annoyed. Eaton took a step toward me, his right hand reached for my shoulder. I moved. My left ripped at his wrist, my right tore at his neck. In one movement I slammed him against the wall. "Now, mister, don't ever do anything funny like that again!"

With contempt I released my hold on the photographer. His eyes were burning savagely at me, but he didn't move. He stood there, his chest heaving in large swallows of air, and the muscles of his chest were like solid steel.

"Now," I said in a pleasant voice, finding it hard to keep my eyes away from Sherry's naked body. The woman was gazing at me with open amazement and admiration in her face. "Let's be friendly. I want to know about Linda Harryington, and you better come out with some answers!"

Eaton didn't say anything.

Sherry laughed, a low throaty laugh that vibrated through her body like she was getting an electric shock.

"Look at him!" she cried. "Scared stiff." She laughed, then added: "Well, not so stiff, I guess. That figures!"

Eaton sprang like a coiled spring had snapped in two. He leaped toward Sherry.

I moved, just in time. He was just about to hit her across the face, when my hand whipped his shoulder around and my right fist slammed out across his face. His head snapped back and he slumped in my grip.

For a moment I looked at the man, surprised at what had happened and then slowly my fingers released his shoulder and he slid down onto the floor.

Sherry was standing there in the middle of the room, a hand over her lips, her eyes wide with horror and surprise. But her whole body was tense, flushed, as if right at the peak of an orgasm.

"Now what?" I asked, dazed.

She shook herself and then said: "He deserved that!"

"What's with him?"

"Quick tempered and a hot head!" She shrugged and her breasts shrugged, too. "Thinks he's a tough guy."

She looked at me with wide-eye admiration. "Boy, man, you really whacked him. God, you're strong as an ox! What'd I'd give to have you doing you guess what with me in a nice, large, lush bed!"

With that, Sherry walked across the room, disappeared into a kitchen and then returned a few moments later with a small pot of water which she threw in the unconscious man's face. Then she bent over, presenting a nicely shaped and exciting fanny in my direction, patted Jay Eaton's face. "Come on, hon, it's all right...all right. Baby, baby...I'm sorry. Little ol" Sherry can fix you're hurt pride."

Slowly the man's eyes opened. He recoiled from her.

"We're sorry. He didn't know about us," Sherry told him. "I wouldn't want him to hurt you."

Eaton snapped to his feet, rubbed his chin and looked at me. "That's some right!"

"Next time, don't try hitting a woman when I'm around!"

Jay Eaton shook his head and then smiled crookedly. "I guess I deserved that. You cut into a session, I don't like to be interrupted when I'm taking pictures."

"Okay, we'll forget it!" I offered generously, extending my hand.

He ignored my hand, but grinned boyishly. "I'm really sorry about this. I don't normally fly off like that...well, not all the time." I looked at Sherry, who shrugged and appeared puzzled. Jay Eaton looked like a number one prime suspect. Too prime!

"About Linda Harryington," I suggested.

"I took pictures of her for Peters" rag-mags. We knew each other for about a year. Nothing more. I didn't kill her, if that's what you mean. Sure, I have a temper! But that's something different. I don't go around knocking off my models."

"She wasn't a professional model!" I pointed out.

"That has nothing to do with it. She was good material, and enjoyed having pictures taken of her. She got real hot, like sexy-hot. She wouldn't pose for anybody else. There was a good demand for her pics. So...would I cool it? She didn't charge a dime! Just for kicks. Hell, she didn't need the money, I did. So she was helping me out a little. Actually, helped me in getting new contacts, and with the Peters" outfit, too. Oh, I'd been doing pics for them before, with her the price went double. Right word at the right time and all that. Hell, what would I have to kill her for? She was a golden, red-hot cow, I mean...money. Money in my jeans. So hot she burned the negs before they were exposed to her! Why'd I kill her?"

"I never suggested that!"

"Oh, come on...Sherry told me all about you!" Eaton said. "I was expecting you."

"And...why the riot act?"

"I forgot! When I'm taking pictures...well, I get

in another world, forget everything."

"Where were you on the night of the murder?"

"Walking the streets. I do that sometimes."

"Down by her beach house?"

"Hell, I don't even know where her beach house is! I never knew about it until...reading the papers about what happened. I can't prove anything, if that's what you mean!" Eaton walked over to the lamps, turned them off one at a time. "No sense in burning them out."

"How intimate was your relationship with Linda?" I asked, watching Sherry's expression. She didn't blink.

"In the first place, pal," Eaton sighed, "that's private...even if there was anything between us. That hasn't anything to do—"

"With it?" I finished for him. "Hell it doesn't! Motive, buster!"

"Motive, hell!" He stared evenly at me, but there was just a suggestion of emotion in his eyes, veiled over emotion.

I shrugged, lighted a cigarette. "You're a busy man, maybe I better come back some other time! How about it?"

My eyes went instinctively to Sherry.

Sherry shrugged. "I could take a walk, while you boys do the talking, if it'll embarrass you, Jay."

"I have nothing more to say. I've told all there is to tell. I can't prove where I was, but I didn't kill her. No motive."

"A fight?"

"A fight! Hell, man, I might get all wound up but...wasn't she found in her beach house? Wasn't she killed in the middle of the night?"

69

"In the morning, sometime between four and seven, according to the police reports!" I corrected.

"Well, I don't take pictures that time of night! And I don't get mad, unless I'm taking pictures." He grinned boyishly again. "I'm really a nice, easy going guy."

"Sure you are!" I turned, opening the door. "But I think you would be smart in staying around, in case the police get ideas about questioning you. I'm only one step in front of them."

"Which way would I run? No place to go anyway!" He gave me that smile again and shrugged.

I closed the door behind me and walked down the hall. As I walked into the late afternoon sun, my mind was whirling around and around at what had happened in Eaton's apartment. His actions had been suspicious, maybe a little too much so. If the police got hold of him, they would write out a warrant for his arrest on the spot. Manhandling a woman. That really pissed me off.

Once in the car I looked at the list of names. There were six more names to look up. Two women. Mary Jenkins and Dora Norton. Instinctively, I picked one of the women, deciding that would be far more interesting than another man. Maybe it was the sight of Sherry's naked body that had sparked a desire to talk to a female. Maybe it was mere animal interest.

Several things I'd learned about Linda. One, she ran hot and cold, depending on the guy, bar and situation. Two, she had a string of lovers, some of which she helped. Three, she got kicks from having naked pictures taken of her and published in magazines. Four, the crowd she ran around with was wild. Sherry had told me enough about Linda to spark an automatic interest in this crowd. Sherry was possibly a prime example of what kind of ladies Linda liked to be around. Ann Harrington was a good example. What would the other's show?

Anyway, I needed a change of setting.

Mary Jenkins lived in the Hollywood Hills. The scenic view from the Hollywood Hills in the evening is one of those beautiful settings that send lovers up among the winding roads to spend several romantic hours in quiet intimacy. Every major town has such a place; this was Hollywood's.

The house that went with Mary Jenkins" address was plush, large, expensive looking. I parked the car and then walked up the stone pathway winding up through beautifully arranged greenery and flowers. Finally I came to the porch and rang the bell. After a moment, a tall, stuffy looking man opened the door and looked out. His tailored uniform identified him as a butler.

"Yes, sir?"

"I wish to speak to Miss Jenkins."

His eyebrows went up and then he said: "I'm sorry, but she isn't in."

"When do you expect her?"

"I don't really know, sir." His voice had a sharp edge of contempt in it.

"Do you expect her home tonight?"

"I really couldn't say."

"What can you say?" I snapped back, angrily.

"Sir?" That eyebrow went up again and then the door slammed shut in my face. I was tempted to ring again until he opened it, then give him a knuckle sandwich, but decided it wasn't worth the time and energy.

Fuming, cursing under my breath, I returned to the car and decided I'd had enough for today.

Twenty minutes later I parked the car in my garage and then went up to the apartment I've rented for well over five years in a plush section of Hollywood, just off the Sunset Strip.

Opening the door, I stepped in and then froze to a standstill.

Sitting on my sofa, her legs crossed, a smile playing on her lips, was a tall lovely redhead. For a moment I could only think two things: what the hell was she doing in my apartment and then, where had I seen her before.

I remembered the latter almost the same time she introduced herself. I'd seen her at the Peters Publications office. The lovely, seductive receptionist.

"Hello, Mr. Maxton. I'm Mary Jenkins."

CHAPTER VII.

I closed the door, slowly, letting my eyes run over the full extent of Mary Jenkins' figure, which was well stacked in the right places. I remembered the subtle exchange at the publication's office.

"How'd you get in?"

"Simple matter. Your manager was quite understanding. I said you were supposed to meet me here and that you'd told me to talk to him, if you hadn't arrived yet. He asked the business I had with you, and when I said private and offered a large size tip for his trouble, he merely laughed off the money and said he guessed it would be all right with you." She grinned from ear to ear. "A girl can get things done, if she really wants to...and is willing to show off a little of herself." Mary Jenkins's eyes went instinctively to her thrusting neckline that was quite nicely revealed by a low cut V, which gave an excellent full view of large, creamy breasts. She was on eye-catching display.

"So...what's the pitch?" I asked, still standing by the door, as if ready to jump out of the apartment. Actually I was still dazed with surprise. I'd been run off looking for her, and here she was, in my apartment, waiting to see me. Why?

"You wanted information about Linda Harryington. I can give you a lot!" Her smile moved wide, revealing even white teeth. Her eyes glided along my form as if attempting to burn the clothing off my body.

Every woman connected with Linda was outright hot. Brazen.

"Why didn't you tell me that...at the office?" I asked, walking across the room to the divider I used as a bar.

"I couldn't."

"Oh, why?"

"You'll understand...after I've told you a few things I know."

"Want a drink?" I offered, pulling out a bottle of Scotch.

"I could use one, thanks."

I poured two stiff drinks and then handed her one. As she took it, her fingers touched mine for only a moment. They were warm and soft and much too inviting. Our eyes met for a moment and then she looked away, took a sip of her drink, and then leaned back against the sofa. The pose was such that it accented her shapely body, breasts. Women always know how to pose in a seductive manner; sometimes I wonder what they actually think about men—probably laugh at how obvious we are.

"Well, what about Linda?" I inquired, making it a point not to sit down next to her. It would be hard enough to keep my attention on what she said, from across the room; if I were close enough to touch, that would have been the end of the question and answer session.

Mary Jenkins was completely different from either Linda or Sherry. Linda had been a ball of energy, alive, important, but also sensitive and had the little girl appeal. Sherry Anderson was one of those cheap bleached blondes, tough, hard, and out for only one kind of life; she was a stripper and played the part all the way!

Mary Jenkins was a subtle flirt. She was seductive, but at the same time had a certain amount of reserved control. Her body was a little rounder than Sherry's, larger and taller than Linda's. Yet, what was even more interesting was the unexpected why she'd been earlier. The subtle office exchange, her business-like manner spiced with the mere suggestion of interest was in bold contrast to her appearance here, in my apartment. I decided that I kinda liked Mary Jenkins" style. But then, it was pretty hard not to like such a lovely woman.

She looked at me for along time before speaking. Finally she stretched out her long legs and then took another sip of her Scotch.

"Where should I start?"

"From the beginning," I said, feeling that was all I had said all day.

"A good Scotch," she announced, looking into the glass in her delicate hand. "I needed a drink. A long day at the office."

Her eyes met mine again, and there was that subtle interest burning there. The expression was both intriguing and amusing, as if she were thinking other thoughts than those centered around Linda Harryington.

"You're quite an attractive man," Mary suddenly announced, smiling. She ran her fingers through the long folds of her hair that flowed over her shoulders.

"That wasn't what we were going to talk about," I pointed out, shaken by the suggestive smile, and action of her hand through her hair. It was as if she were mentally wondering the same things I was beginning to wonder. Here we were, in an apartment, alone, drinking, the evening already settling down upon us; two adults with an obviously healthy outlook about life and sex. Sometimes two people will meet and something clicks; it doesn't have to be emotional, and it doesn't have to be serious. There was a class and warmth about Mary Jenkins that reached out and grabbed at a man, when she turned the furnace on full blast. She was blasting away with those deep green eyes.

"What's wrong," she asked, lightly, "with pointing out the obvious? You're attractive. That's all. Does it bother you for a woman to offer compliments?

I chuckled, offered: "Because it's obvious?"

She laughed, throwing back her head, giving me a beautiful view of her creamy white neck. She became more beautiful the longer I looked at her. Suddenly I wished I had sat next to her. Talking about Linda seemed as far out of place as making conversation about the cartoons in the middle of a racy bedroom scene.

She sobered, sipped her drink once again and then became all business. "I met Linda about six months ago. We started running around in the same crowd. Well...no, I'll say, she started running around in the same crowd I was. All the same, anyway. She was seeing a lot of Ned Peters, among other guys: Jay Eaton, Charlie Manners, and Walter Stevens, to name a few. She made a hit with all of them. I must say, in all honesty, she didn't hit it off so well with the girls. Dora Norton was knocked, but good, when Linda started turning on the charm for Walt. Dora and Walt were like that!" Mary crossed her fingers to make the point. "Serious things were in the offering before Linda came along. Linda blinked her eyes and Walt jumped right into her lap, so to speak. That was Linda!"

Mary took a breath, a sip of Scotch, finished the rest of the liquor in another long swallow and then extended her glass towards me. "Another?"

"Why not?" I finished my drink, stood and took her glass as she continued.

"Linda started playing the boys against one another. You see...well, let me explain something. There's a group that gathers socially...artists, writers, photographers, guys who do business with Ned Peters. Then there's the fringe element. You know, like the partners who are not artistic. Dora, Larry, Henry Davis. Dora for Walt, then she spun off into Sherry's territory by snapping up Henry but that didn't worry Sherry, because she has a thing for all the guys. She strips because it's fun! That's the kind of girl Sherry is. Well, anyway, like the story goes, there was a lot of switching, some for fun, some for revenge, some for loneliness. Ann Harryington got in the action a couple of times, but nothing too involved. Ann and Linda seemed to have known each other long before getting related. Ann's one of those girls who likes to marry for money. Everybody but her husband knows the truth, but that's nobody's business, anyway! Hell, who wouldn't marry into that kind of money?"

I handed her the stiff drink of Scotch and she paused long enough to give me one of her subtle looks. A chill rushed over my spine like somebody had run hot ice along it.

"The point is, Linda made a lot of enemies."

"I know that," I stated, standing over her, not wanting to return to the chair I'd been sitting in on the opposite side of the room, and afraid to sit down next to her.

"She made some excellent enemies. Jay Eaton, Dora, Frank Peters "

"Frank Peters?"

"That's the point. That's why I couldn't talk to you at the office. He'd fire me if I told you this. But...well, actually even though I don't need the job, I want it. Frank was Linda's lover, too. She flaunted herself at him, and kept giving him trouble about his son. That's why she cooled it with Ned. I think Ned was the only one who didn't really know what kind of...well, bitch she was, if you'll excuse the expression."

"Do you think Frank—"

"Killed her?"

"Well, he apparently had a motive."

"Frank is fifty-five, he's in love with, was in love with, Linda...but come on, you surely don't think he would have killed her!"

"I don't have any exact ideas, yet. I'm just asking questions, trying to find out who might be the most likely. When that happens...well, I'll start putting on the pressure. Have any real ideas?"

Her eyes sparkled and the point of her tongue

moistened her lush red lips. "About what?"

"About Linda's murder."

"Oh. That. Well, I was thinking something else. Sorry."

"I don't believe you."

"Well, why not? Don't you think I'm an...honest woman?"

Suddenly puzzled, taken by surprise by her question I offered: "I never said I doubted you."

"You said you didn't believe me...well, I was thinking how nice you look standing there over me like some demon god, who can't get enough of looking and—"

Suddenly I felt embarrassed, naked. I had been staring down at her like I wanted to fairly devour her with more than my eyes.

"You don't seem to take all this very seriously!" I pointed out, finding it hard to keep my eyes from the low cut of her neckline.

"I take it very seriously. Why else do you think I'm here?" she offered in a throaty voice.

"I wouldn't be able to guess in a million years!" I threw back, knowing exactly what was on her little hot mind.

After a moment of silence, I asked: "Exactly what kind of group was it you and Linda ran around with?"

"Like I told you, modern. We believed that we might as well get our kicks before it was all over! Good thing Linda lived to the hilt. Don't you think? And anyway, the world might come to a quick end. War and all that."

"Oh, come on, you surely didn't believe that the world was going to come to an end?"

"Why not?" Her smile was mocking. "After all, all it takes is a crazy man on either side and, bang!" Her hands slapped together, making a loud smacking sound.

"How about another?" She indicated the glass on the lamp stand next to the sofa.

"You really slap it down, don't you?"

"Down the hatch and into my lovely little belly and shakes like jelly." She laughed at that. "Sorry. Just showing off my literary demeanor. Okay, I'm being silly. Scotch scotches me like that! But I love it. I can get you a whole case, without even feeling it!" she pointed out with an innocent bright smile.

"I didn't mean that. Just an observation." I picked up the glass. She grabbed hold of my arm, her fingers were hot and moist on my flesh.

"Make it strong?" she, requested. "And stiff! Don't water it down."

Some how she made those words have a very sexual content to them.

"How strong can it get?" I countered, looking down at her.

"Like…your arm. Golly gee, you're really like steel!"

Suddenly the whole situation was beginning to wear on my nerves. Either we were going to rack it, or not. She squeezed my arm.

"It can get pretty strong, Stan!" The way she said my name was like a physical caress. "The stronger the better. I could use a little relaxation. Been a hard day at the office. And not the way I like it hard."

A shiver rushed through her, and she hugged her arms.

80

"Okay, baby! One strong one coming up." Mary Jenkins laughed at that, and I wasn't quite sure exactly why, and wasn't about to ask. Some ladies can have pretty risqué minds; and she was quite obviously one hell of a sophisticated, smart woman.

This time I sat down next to her, and Mary did the unexpected, by throwing her legs up, and laying them across mine in a very casual intimate fashion as if we were old friends, lovers, intimates. She stretched out, propping her head against the back of the sofa. It seemed an awkward position, but showed a good thrusting breast/

"Mary, could there be any other reason somebody might have killed Linda, other than jealousy?" I offered, taking a swallow of my own drink.

"Why?"

"What about Phil Baxtar?"

"What about him? Linda was engaged to Phil, but that's as far as the relationship went. It was an arranged engagement, without any real emotional attention put to it. They were to get married, but...well, it seems they both were having their own private affairs."

"Ever meet Baxtar?"

"Once."

"What's he look like?"

"A dream, only a little more heavy than I like them. Not that he's chunky, just that I like the tall, muscular type. He looks weak. Smart as all get-out, but I wouldn't want to cross him!"

"Maybe Linda crossed him?" I suggested, finding it suddenly impossible to keep my fingers off her legs. I ran a caress from her ankle up to her knee.

She writhed slightly, said: "That feels good!"

Then she asked: "How could Linda cross him?"

"I don't know."

"Neither do I. I don't know much more, anyway...if you must know the truth. There just isn't that much to tell about Linda. She was like the rest of us, free swinging! Anything for kicks!" She suddenly sat up, looked probingly at me, asked: "What kind of man are you?"

The question startled me. I hadn't quite expected it. Totally out of context.

"Well?" she pushed, caressing my shoulder.

"That all depends on what you mean," I said carefully, finding it hard to control my voice.

Her hand slipped under my jacket, caressed the hard chest muscle which flexed instinctively to the touch.

"You're so damned hard!" she announced. "I like men with muscles!"

I could hardly keep from laughing. Then I saw the expression in her eyes and there wasn't anything to laugh about.

Her whole face was transposed into a lusty expression. Her eyes half-lidded, her full lips parted, moist, as if waiting to be kissed, her creamy white neck throbbing as if her heart were bursting inside her heaving chest. Suddenly I reached for her and our lips met, hot, and open. Her tongue greedily surged deep into my mouth, then retreated. I probed the depths of her wide mouth, feeling the heat blast up through me like a furnace gone wild. She shifted in my arms, her hands caressed the back of my neck, her breasts, soft cushions, pressed tight against my chest, as the kiss took on all the proportions of an atomic blast.

After a moment we came up for air.

"Stan...oh, I've been wanting to do that ever since I saw you at the office. Some men do that to me. Some men, I look at and get all chilly all over. I can't help myself. Something happens...almost uncontrollable to me. Oh, Stan, Stan," she murmured into my ear, caressing it with her words, her soft lips.

That kind of punishment no man can take and still call himself a man. Beyond the fact that Mary was one hell of a sexy woman, after all that I'd gone through that day, Sherry's offer, her complete nudity in Eaton's apartment, and now Mary's obviously blatant offer, it was too much to take without grabbing the prize being given.

"Okay, I guess you know what you're doing!" I said, standing and pulling her up to her feet.

"If you mean, I'm over twenty-one, and know what I want...I guess you're right!" she laughed, squeezing my hand with her fingers. We moved to the bedroom, closing the door behind us.

Mary came into my arms, yielding, trembling, desperate with wanting, overwhelming in her demanding attack that left no room for subtle build-ups. The kiss lasted as long as our breath needed no refilling. Then, gasping, Mary backed away toward the bed. I watched as she slipped out of her dress and then released her bra and dropped it to the floor. She smiled settling down onto the bed and reached out for me.

I didn't need a second invitation. The blood was throbbing at my temples like hot wine. All I could think about was taking this luscious female in my arms and making love to every silken inch of her body.

In moments I was undressed and in those willing arms.

We kissed again, this time the full impact hitting me like a charging train was knocking me a mile down track. My hands moved over her in lightening caresses, my lips feasted on her throat, her ears, her shoulders, until she pushed me downwards into the full, supple mound of her lovely breasts. After that the raging furnace went completely wild. She writhed as if possessed by some devil that wanted out, but couldn't escape. The soft, low animal gasps which choked from her tortured throat spurred me onto the stunning heights of love-making. Suddenly she was more than just a hot chick wanting a thrill. She was an expert lover, a Goddess of Passion, which inspired the most potent power of a man's resources, that demanded the full extent of his ability to caress and kiss and feast upon the banquet of her lovely body. At the rate we were going it was impossible to slow down to a point where it would take the long time, the long route of loving; it never let up; it rushed to a frantic start and then picked up pace. When the ultimate actions joined our bodies in the final explosive union, I never was quite sure. Suddenly we were one throbbing unit, and then, like a rocket falling into the atmosphere, we burned through the final moments of ecstasy until all that was left was exhaustion, the bittersweet beauty of the aftermath of our union.

CHAPTER VIII.

As I lay there, semi-conscious, my thoughts drifted away from Mary Jenkins, and traveled over the territory that I'd covered since taking on this case.

Several things had happened. Somebody had had me worked over. Why? To get me off the case. But nobody had done anything after that. When would the next attempt be made to stop me? In what shape would it come? And who had done it? Somebody with money; somebody with enough money to buy hoods to do the dirty work. Phil Baxtar, the shadowy man in Linda's life? Reasonable. But it could also have been Ralph Harryington. I ignored that thought and tried to think about other things.

Mary moved on the bed next to me, then I felt her weight lift from the bed.

My eyes opened.

She was reaching for her clothing that had been left on the floor by the bed.

"Going?" I asked, sitting up.

"Might as well," she announced. "I live at home and have questions to answer now and then. The family gets worried."

"I thought you were a big girl?"

"I'm a big girl, but I live at home because it's easier that way!" Mary pointed out.

Suddenly I had the impression she was lying. *But why?*

"Don't go. Call and say you were detained," I suggested, puffing her into my arms.

She let me kiss her and then gently pushed away. "Really, I must be going. It's already late. Anyway, we've done the bit...and—"

"And you leave after the first round."

Mary Jenkins laughed and then pulled on her bra. "That first round was just too much! Too good! I'll come back...again, if you want!"

Suddenly I decided the best thing was to play it silent, let her have the lead, a long, long lead.

"Again, some time, then," I said, returning to the bed and lying down. I watched her dress, delighting in the gentle movement of her breasts, body, as she went through the actions of pulling on her dress and arranging it around her figure.

"Well," she said, "it's been really · fun!" She stepped closer and leaned over, planting one soft, moist kiss on my lips, then straightened and looked down at me. "You know, Stan, you really are damned good. I wish I could stay!" She frowned and then shrugged. "But some times a girl has to do...things she doesn't want to. Maybe that's why all of us flash around a lot, escape from responsibilities."

With that she started out of the room. At the door she turned, blew me a kiss and then disappeared.

The moment the front door was closed, I leaped

86

to my feet, and dressed like I had aunts driving me wild. There wasn't any time to arrange anything, in fact, as it turned out, I forgot to strap on my .38 revolver. The moment my pants were on, I tucked in my shirt while walking through the living room. Grabbing my coat from a chair, I opened the front door and walked carefully outside.

Luck was with me, for once.

Mary Jenkins was getting into a sports car across the street. I moved along the shadows and then slipped into the front seat of my own car. I watched through the rear-view mirror as Mary's car pulled away from the curb and down the road.

Firing the engine, I shot the car out of the garage and then hurriedly turned in the direction Mary Jenkins had taken.

The moment she had used the excuse it was important that she be home, to keep the family from worrying, I knew something smelled. Mary Jenkins wasn't the type to be dependent on the family, the very fact that she had gotten a job at the Peters' publishing firm proved her independence. She was up to something; and I meant to find out.

As I followed her car through the town, I kept thinking about the little scene in the living room and where it had ended in another room.

The more I thought about it, the more convinced I became that it was a set-up job. Why had she seduced me? Because I was so impossibly attractive that she couldn't stand it? Possibly! And Santa Claus is a monkey from the moon. Maybe for some other reason. But what? To see that I stayed at a certain place for a certain amount of time? To keep me away from some other location? To...what? That didn't make any sense, so I killed that line of fire.

The drive took us through Beverly Hills, down Sunset Boulevard and then into Bel Aire. Here we turned up a side road and into the Santa Monica Hills. A short ride led to a large two story white house in front of which Mary Jenkins parked.

I drove on past and then, after rounding a bend in the road, turned and then parked the car.

Getting out, I ran down the road until I came opposite the place where the woman had parked.

Mary Jenkins was just walking into the house. The door was closed by some tall fairly good-looking man.

I went to the mail box, hoping there would be a name on it. Only the address, which I quickly jotted down in a small notebook I keep in my pocket for such emergencies.

Returning to my car, I started it and then drove around the bend in the road, parked again, just in sight of Mary's car.

I lighted a cigarette and sat, waiting.

My thoughts drifted several times, running the conversations I'd had with Linda's past friends. The only solid conclusions I came to were that Linda swung and that some jealous love might have killed her, possibly Jay Eaton, who had the temper; or Frank Peters, who might have had a good motive But every other person on the list seemed to have the same possible motive. The simple fact was that I had gotten no closer to solving the case than I'd been in the beginning. I'd merely learned a little about the people on the list, and their relations with Linda, and what she did for some of them. But nothing, as yet, that might even, in the smallest way, really point a finger toward any one person.

I smoked my pack of cigarettes down to zero and still Mary Jenkins didn't come out of the house.

I continued to wait, wondering what the hell I was doing there. Actually there might not have been anything to her leaving my apartment so suddenly, or to her coming to this Bel Aire house, instead of going home. Maybe it was as innocent as a mere intimate relationship between another man and herself. Yet that inner, negative, hunch kept eating away at my mind.

It was well past three in the morning by the time Mary Jenkins returned to her car. I had almost dozed off. The minute she started the engine, I turned the key in the ignition, waited until she was well down the road and then started my car.

Mary followed a return route toward Hollywood, taking her time, as if in no hurry. Finally she turned up into the Hollywood Hills and I realized that she was going home at last. Instead of following her, I headed toward my own apartment.

The next morning I was awakened by the ringing of my phone. My brain was still foggy from lack of sleep as I picked up the receiver.

"Stan Maxton?"

"Yes."

"Lt. Hanson."

"What's it this time? Roses?"

"Another body. We want you down at the station for questioning."

"Who is it this time?" I shot back, fully awake.

"Mary Jenkins," he announced.

THE SEX CULT MURDERS, BY CHARLES NUETZEL

CHAPTER IX.

I looked at Lt. Hanson's hard features and shouted: "What the hell's the idea of calling me down this time?"

All the way to the police station my heart was in my mouth. How the hell had that happened? Who would kill Mary Jenkins? Why? Two girls I'd slept with, and then the next morning they were discovered dead. Three would be the charm.

Hanson's face clouded as he slammed back into his chair. He looked up at the ceiling, pressed the fingers of each hand against one another and then sighed.

"I don't know where you fit, this time, but she was involved with Linda. There's a connection."

"Smart!" I snapped back.

"Don't get funny, Maxton. I could pull your license!" the man warned, snapping upwards, glaring at me. "Now, tell me what you were doing yesterday."

"Passing the time of day!"

"Look, smart guy, I know you were running checks, talking to people. Don't try wiggling out of this!" His face was beat red. "What's with you guys, anyway? Read too many detective novels? Think you have to be the hard boiled private dick? Hell, just try once to see it our way." He tapped the index finger of his right hand, and said: "First, you were out there in the beach house with Linda Harrington, probably the night of the murder! Two, Mary Jenkins was in your apartment last night. You followed her to a Bel Air address, waited until she left, followed her to the road leading to the Jenkins' house in the Hollywood Hills, and then returned home. My man stayed long enough to be quite sure you were going to bed this time, and then about six this morning was called off your trail. That's when we got the report on Miss Jenkins. Okay, now, are you ready to start cooperating?"

I was stunned for a full minute, unable to say anything. It hadn't occurred to me that the police put a tail on my activities.

"Surprised, Maxton?" Hanson asked. "Well, up until last night you were the turkey for the raffle. Now...we don't know for sure!"

"Why didn't you arrest me?"

"Motive, and reputation. You have been highly spoken for by Captain Turner! Otherwise we might have locked you up, but good." Hanson stood, pulled out a cigar from his breast jacket pocket and then lighted it. Surrounded by smoke, he said: "So...what do you know about Mary Jenkins?"

I considered, then said: "Nothing. She works for Ned Peters. She ran in the same gang as Linda. She came to the apartment to talk about Linda."

"What about?"

"Things she couldn't say with Ned Peters

92

around."

"What?"

"Generally that his father was running around with Linda."

Lt. Hanson made an ugly face, looked at the lighted end of his cigar and then said: "So?"

"So...another piece in the puzzle."

"Why do you think she was killed?" Hanson fired.

"Hell, I don't even know how she was killed, or when. I don't know enough about her to even make an educated guess. Maybe the guy she was visiting last night," I offered.

"Wouldn't check out. Her uncle. Larry Sherman, mother's brother. No motive! They were as close as daughter and father."

"Why'd she visit him that late at night?" I asked, more to myself than Hanson.

"I'm asking the questions!" Hanson told me in a hard voice. Then he said more softly, "I couldn't tell you! Even if I could. I've been asking that question myself."

"Maybe she was meeting somebody else there?" I suggested.

"Why?" he asked. "Who?"

"I couldn't possibly guess." Only suddenly I was beginning to make some pretty good ones silently to myself.

Hanson was thoughtful for a moment. "Maxton, do me a favor and tell what you have found out about Linda Harryington? I think there might be a connection."

"Sorry...but the only thing I know is that she managed to please a lot of guys in bed, and that Jay

Eaton has a violent temper, and possibly the only motive was jealousy, but from any number of people. I'd eliminate Bill Carver, that was casual, and she was helping him along in his career. Ned Peters seems to have been the only one who wasn't shacking up with her...he was surprised to find out that she actually lived a racy life. Nothing on Sherry Anderson that I know of. Nor was there on Mary Jenkins. I understand Dora Norton was knocked out because Linda took Walter Stevens away for keeps but...apparently Dora wasn't the kind of girl to hold a long standing hate, she racked it with some other guy, I can't remember who. Names get confusing. I haven't seen Dora, and don't know anything other than what I've heard. Does that tell you anything?"

Hanson laughed. "Nothing! At least you aren't doing any better than the police department. That's a kick in the head for you private dicks! But I'll give you one you apparently don't know. Dora Norton was in San Francisco the night of Linda's murder, so I'd say she'd be out, in any case. For another fact, whoever killed Linda had to be a man! We're sure of that!"

"Why?"

"A witness said they saw a man leaving the beach house about six in the morning.

"They apparently saw you and Linda arrive, earlier, and assumed it was you who left at six." Hanson grinned. "Swallow that one down! In any case, you're still number one, as far as the evidence goes. But between you and me, I don't think you had reason enough."

"Thanks!" I said, feeling a chill rush through me. If they found a motive and it was highly possi-

94

ble that they might, considering the close relationship Linda and myself had had years before, Hanson
might change his mind. At least he wasn't pointing
the finger at me for the Mary Jenkins murder.

After a moment Hanson made a movement with
his right hand, and said: "Get out of here!"

"Tailing me?"

"If I say no, you wouldn't believe me, so why
ask the question?" Hanson offered.

I shrugged and left.

Once in my car, I decided the first thing to do
was to find out if there was a tail on me, then lose it.

I started the car and headed north, towards the
freeway. In the next twenty minutes I kept up a turning, jazzy course, doubling back on my route and
then when I was sure that no tail could possibly
have kept up, I parked and looked at the list Ann
Harryington had given me.

Dora Norton's name stood out the largest. Partly
because she was a woman, and the women in
Linda's life were hot offerings to any takers, and
partly because she might be able to give me some
more information, mainly about those whom I had
already talked to. The fact that she seemed off the
list as a possible, seemed to make her more likely to
give full accounts. And I was, naturally, curious
concerning her feminine charms. If nothing else she
might be a diversion from the police.

She lived in North Hollywood, a small town that
is growing into a large one, just inside the San Fernando Valley, a few miles north of Hollywood.

Dora lived in a small house, off Burbank Boulevard. When I stepped up to the porch the front door
opened and a cute little dark haired woman stepped

out. She was dressed in a black, cocktail dress, which hugged a bouncy full figure. She couldn't have been over five feet four, just coming to my chin.

She saw me and gasped in surprise. "I'm sorry, but I'm not buying anything, and I'm in a hurry."

"Miss Norton?" I asked. "I'm Stan Maxton." She squinted at me and then took a step backwards as if suddenly frightened.

"You!" she spat out.

"All of me!" I countered. "I wanted to talk to you about—"

"I can't!" she announced, starting to walk past me.

I grabbed hold of her arm, and said: "Can't you please spare a few moments. It could be important."

"For whom? You or me?" she demanded coldly, turning and looking up at me. Her eyes were large and dark brown.

"Probably for you!"

She laughed, softly. "Are you kidding? From what I heard, you are listed on the top!"

"Oh, you've heard about me?"

"A lot. From Sherry. From Mary. In fact, I'm on my way to see Mary Jenkins and—"

"Don't bother, she's dead."

Dora Norton winced as if slapped. For a moment she stood there, staring at me, her expression blank, then the color drained from her deeply tanned face. "You can't mean—"

"She's dead, or the police are pulling my leg!" I announced, reaching out and grabbing hold of her shoulders. For a moment she swayed and then collapsed against me, shaking.

96

Regardless, I couldn't help being aware of the attractiveness of this neat little package of womanhood. I did what I could to comfort her until she finally moved back, away from me. For a moment she looked at the car parked in her driveway and then to the front door.

"Want to talk?" I asked.

"I'm scared," was all Dora said as she stepped past me and opened the door. "Come in."

I followed the woman into the small front room. She dropped into a large red chair and opened her purse. Lighting a cigarette she met my eyes with her lovely eyes.

"What do you want to know?"

"Anything you can tell me."

Silence, then: "I don't know if I should tell you anything."

"Why?"

"That's my business!" She was silent for a long time. Not until she had finished the cigarette and lighted another did she continue. Her hand was shaking, and her lips seemed on the verge of trembling.

"If I wasn't frightened...but things are getting a little out of hand."

She hesitated and I asked: "In what way?"

"First Linda's death, now Mary's. Who is next?" she said, as if it were quite obvious.

"You expect more?"

She nodded.

"Why?"

"That's it...I don't know why, I just know that something has gone wrong, something is backfiring." She snubbed out the cigarette and then lighted another. "You have to understand...the group we've been...free swinging, but emotions ran high. Linda was, well, you might say, high queen of the fair." Dora laughed bitterly. "She took over fast. Made very fast moves into every man's bed."

"Along with Walter Stevens?"

"Walt, too."

"Why would anybody want to kill Linda, and then Mary?"

"Not jealousy, in the way you might think."

My ears went on instant alert, for the first time it looked as if another view-point was about to slap out some important information.

"We were more than just a group of swingers. You might say we were a club of sorts. And Larry Sherman was high priest, in a way. No, not in the way you think. You might say he organized us. Maybe that's not quite right. I'll start from the beginning.

"Larry Sherman is about forty-five, the younger brother of Mary Jenkins' mother. He was...well a little of a playboy, with a difference. He didn't play for virgins, he played for kicks. And I mean that with a large K! It was more than just getting girls in bed with him. I came across Larry about three years ago. He was a friend of Frank Peters' and I...well, modeled for the magazines. I was in the office one day and Larry made a pass. He'd been looking at one of my pictures and said he thought I was really something. His pass was actually innocent enough in itself. He asked me out to lunch and cocktails. Well, I never was one to turn down such an of-fer...so we ended up at his Bel Air home, a private lunch with all the trimmings, including desert and—

"

She raised an eyebrow. "Surprised that I'm willing to talk about it?"

I guess my face had given me away. "Let's say, the women in your group were certainly far from bashful."

"Hell, I don't mind admitting it. I like a good tumble. There aren't many! And most girls in my profession are real squares. They don't really dig real kicks. You have to search long before finding such a swinging group. Well, as it turned out, we hit it off pretty well, Larry and me. He invited me to a party for that weekend, which I expected to turn out to be private, but it was actually a real live party, where everybody ended up naked as they were born, running around the large house and indoor pool. It started with Sherry Anderson giving a private showing, one that stripped down completely. Linda took the floor after that and attempted to rival Sherry, and I guess she did a pretty good job...but that was Linda for you. I stripped willingly, anxious to get some of the stares. The other girls followed and the men didn't waste any time joining us. From then on it was nudist kicks like they don't have at those sun camps! The party roared all night Saturday and into late Sunday. At the time I was going with Walter Stevens and—"

"Didn't you feel a little...well, reluctant to—"

"Have a ball? Nothing was serious, yet, between Walt and me." She shrugged. "Anyway, what difference does it make? I didn't return to the party house for about six months, anyway. By that time I'd gotten serious with Walt, and I thought it was a two-way thing. I was invited to a party Frank Peters was giving on New Year's Eve and there we ran into Linda and Mary Jenkins. Linda flicked a breasty chest toward Walt, and that was the end of that!" She stopped for a moment and then continued: "Actually it wasn't quite that fast. In any case, a week later, I learned that Walt had seen Linda, and we were washed up. In the next months I managed to swing with the 'club' group again. That continued...until now. Now I'm frightened. Something's going on and I don't like it."

A shiver rushed over her and then she lowered her eyes to the floor.

"You think some nut is out to chop the women up?" I offered, not quite able to believe that line of reasoning.

"I don't know," she told me in a small, frightened voice.

"I can't see how that could be..."

I was thoughtful for a moment.

Mary Jenkins had gone over to see her uncle after having talked to me. Could there be some connection to what we had talked about and her sudden trip to Sherman's place, and her death? I wondered, trying to remember everything that had been said in our conversation. I couldn't think of anything offering an answer to my question.

"Would there be any possible reason for Sherman to kill Mary Jenkins?"

"Are you kidding?" Dora exploded. "They were so close...they could have been daughter and father."

Fine relationship, I thought, considering that the uncle had been quite willing to let his "daughter" live it up in a depraved club at which he was king pin.

Suddenly I realized I wanted to talk to Larry Sherman; and fast!

Standing, I said: "Thanks, you've been a help."

Her eyes turned to mine, pleading, frightened. "I'm scared."

Then she stood, came into my arms. Just like that.

"Look, baby, there's nothing to be frightened about. I don't think this is a killer run wild."

She trembled against me like a little child, only she wasn't a child. The large, hefty bounce of her breasts shook against me, building an instinctive fire. I knew if I stood there a moment longer I would stay for a lot longer. Plus the last two women I'd slept with had ended up dead-meat. I wasn't anxious to add a third to the list.

Gently pushing her away, I went to the door, opened it and stepped out onto the porch.

Then I walked to the car, started the engine and headed for Bel Air.

THE SEX CULT MURDERS, BY CHARLES NUETZEL

CHAPTER X.

I was ushered into a small comfortable den that had several book cases on one wall and a desk on the opposite one. What I might have expected from Larry Sherman wasn't what followed. In the first place I had a mental picture of a middle aged man who delighted in seduction of young women half his age. A man who was a little pudgy and balding early.

Well, as it turned out, Larry Sherman was quite tall, well proportioned, strikingly good looking and had thick wavy hair. There was a thin moustache on his upper lip, and as he smiled his teeth revealed themselves to be almost beautiful. I could easily understand why a woman like Dora Norton would have gone for him; in fact, it was hard to understand why she hadn't gone serious.

His smile was warm, but his eyes looked tired, tortured.

"What can I do for you, Mr. Maxton?" he offered, taking my hand in his large one.

The handshake was that of two men sizing each other up.

"Won't you sit down, have a cigar?" He extended a leather covered box.

"Thanks, but no." I pulled out a pack of Luddes and lighted up.

"You'll have to excuse me...if I get disconnected...Mary was pretty close...we were...well, good pals. We saw things pretty much alike. It hits hard."

He lighted a cigar and puffed, then took an unexpected deep drag. Then he leaned back in his chair and threw his long legs onto the top of the desk. "I guess you've come over to ask about Mary, and Linda?"

"Something like that! Any connection? I mean between their deaths?" I watched his face for any reaction. There wasn't even a blink.

"That's an interesting question, Maxton," he admitted lightly. His fingers played with the cigar and for a few moments that held the attention of his deep-set eyes. "You know, she came over here last night...she'd been with you, she said. Seemed to enjoy herself!" His eyes snapped up to mine, there was a twinkle in them. "I'm glad she had one last moment before..." His voice faded out and for a moment he looked away from me. He finally said, "I'm truly sorry."

"I understand."

An awkward silence followed, then finally Sherman swung his legs down off the desk and stared at me. "I'd give you five thousand to find out who did it to her!"

That was an unexpected attack. I blinked and nodded. "Okay, if I find out, I'll let you know...a deal?"

104

"A deal!"

"Now, could you tell me all you know about this little club you have?"

It was his turn to show surprise. He narrowed his eyes and then stood, paced around the desk, went to one of the book shelves and stared at the books as if reading their titles. Finally he sighed: "How'd you find out about that?"

"Let's say it would be better not reveal who told me."

He whipped around, his face was hard, his eyes glaring at me. "Who was it?"

For a moment I hesitated and then made a quick decision. "Mary."

He continued to glare at me for a moment and then seemed to relax, his expression looked relieved.

"Not that there's anything wrong with it. We're all adults and...well, we all like to have a little fun. Actually...well, some people are a little small-minded about it. But...when you consider the broad practice of 'key clubs,' and little games like that...well, we weren't much different from that, except we were all unmarried." He shrugged. "Actually, I think what takes place between two consenting adults is no damned body's business but the people involved. Regardless of what they do!" The words had spat out, harsh, angry. "There are too many prudes who would think sex is just to have babies. That's for the Dark Ages! Some Churches seem to think they should not only dictate to their flock, but to every other flock within reach and every damned person in the world. I'd like to get my hands on them and..."

He broke off, his lips smiled and for the first time I realized that the expression was a well-practiced movement of his facial muscles.

"Well, we're getting off the subject. I guess you want to know about Linda and Mary."

"All...all of them. The whole bit."

He shrugged, sat down in the desk chair again and tapped the long ash from the end of his cigar, his eyes watching my every movement.

"So we get together. I have a lot of money. Actually, I started out pretty well in life. Maybe you've heard of the Sherman Metal Company. Well, that was the Old Man's...and when he died I took it over, worked my ass off and made a few smart moves and found myself even better off. But by that time I was well in my thirties and had a healthy desire for women, lots of women. Some guys are built that way. In any case, I started dropping out of the business world, letting my companies run themselves, and began living off the fat of the land, as they say. When you have money, and contact, you start to find yourself surrounded by women willing to spend evenings alone with you. Later you find there are some who really don't care how they get their kicks. I met Linda that way. I met Sherry that way. Most of the girls in the group."

"I take it there were quite a few outside of Linda, Sherry, Dora and Mary?"

"Quite a few, but they came and went. Those four stayed for a longer time. Like me, and a few others."

"What about Jay Eaton?"

"Don't know him."

"Bill Carver?"

106

"I don't, wait...oh, hell, he's that writer. He came to a party once, stayed for the night, and never came back again. He was with Linda, I think."

"How well did you know Linda?"

"As well as the other girls."

"For kicks?"

"Kicks! I didn't kill her, if that's what you mean."

"Phil Baxtar?"

"He was the shadow in Linda's life. They lived their own private lives. As you know, they were going to get married at some distant time in the future."

"Ann Harryington?"

"We used to know each other."

"Oh?"

"Before she was married to Ralph Harryington. We went out together for some time. Nothing serious, mind you."

"Nothing serious," I repeated thoughtfully. "You stopped seeing her, after she got married to Harryington?"

"Of course," he quickly assured me.

Everything seemed to be going around in circles, giving no clues, giving no real hint that could lead me closer to the murder of Linda Harryington. But, strangely, I couldn't help thinking I was always getting closer and closer to the actual facts.

"You don't have any idea why Linda or Mary were killed?"

He slowly shook his head from side to side. "If I knew...believe me...I wouldn't be standing still." There was a light edge of threat in his voice.

I shrugged. Another blind end.

Slowly I stood. "Thanks. I guess that's it, then. I have a few other people to see before the day is shut down."

He stood, shook hands and then walked out of the room with me.

Twenty minutes later I was talking to a sandy-haired man by the name of Sam Winters. He was one of those few on the list whom I hadn't spoken to and had heard little about. As it turned out, he owned the Hot Spot, which was in evidence the moment I stepped into the one room apartment.

There were posters of Sherry Anderson on the walls, a neon sign in the corner that said:
The Hot Spot.

I questioned him about that, and he quickly admitted having ownership of the place.

On a hunch I asked him about Ann Harryington and Larry Sherman, after the obvious questions about Linda that had given no new information and mentioned nothing about the little private club,

"Oh, Ann and Larry were thick as you could get, before she married Ralph."

"Why the split?"

He frowned. "I couldn't say. He has enough money. Maybe because of Linda, I don't know."

I soon discovered, after short questioning, that he had been at his strip club the night of the murder of Mary Jenkins.

After leaving him I suddenly decided it was time to have a talk with Ann Harryington. Maybe she could give me a little more information. With what I now knew about her, and the involvement between her and Larry Sherman, which she had avoided telling about, I had a hunch she might reveal a new angle to the case. It was quite obvious to me, by now, that running around from one person to another wasn't getting me any closer to answers. Some vital element was missing.

The drive out to the Harryington home was a long study in fighting the late afternoon traffic, which has a habit of pulling up all over the place in Los Angeles. The only thing about traffic jams is that no matter what nothing will move the cars ahead of you. I've always been a strong believer that people making left turns, who wait for the signal to change, should be hung by the necks. By the time I arrived, my nerves were fired raw, my temper controlled by a narrow invisible wall.

I was taken into the drawing room by the butler, who said he would get Mrs. Harryington.

The room was large, with a high ceiling, and contained expensively furnisher. I sat in a low off-white sofa, lighted a cigarette and waited.

Linda had lived here. Ann Harryington had lived here. She had been balling it with Sherman before marrying Ralph Harryington. What had happened to break her off with Sherman? That was question number one. Question number two: did that have anything to do with the murder of Linda Harryington and Mary Jenkins?

It was a new angle, a wild one that didn't make sense. But this was what had brought me to the Harryington home.

After a few minutes Ann Harryington stepped into the room.

She was dressed, surprisingly, in pedal-pushers that hugged around her lush body, and a tight fitting green sweater. On her arms were a couple of bracelets; her hair was loose around her shoulders, like silken black waves; her expression bright, the eyes shining.

"Well, hello big detective Maxton!" The slur of her words revealed she'd been drinking. "How's the big case?"

"Circling around and around."

She smiled and for a moment it almost looked like a pleased smile.

She sat down next to me on the sofa, brought her legs up under her and let her eyes rove over my body. She smiled again, warmly. "You're all right. I really didn't get a good chance to actually notice what a hunk of male flesh you are!"

A standard greeting for the girls in Linda's life. I sighed, tapped an ash into an ash-tray and asked: "What happened between you and Larry Sherman?"

Ann ran fingers casually through her hair. "That's private."

"Tell me about it and I'll tell you how private it is!" I snapped back.

Her eyes lowered to the floor. "That was over a long time ago! Ralph knew all about it."

"Why didn't you mention it before?"

"It wasn't of any importance."

"I think it is!"

Her eyes jerked to mine, there was anger in them, and something else veiled behind the emotion. "What exactly does that mean?"

"You and Sherman knew each other, you were...well, lovers, from what I've heard, and then you wind up marrying Ralph Harryington."

"Didn't you ever hear of love?"

It was hard, but I held back a laugh of contempt.

110

It just didn't seem logical that she would really be in love with Harryington. To me, it was a cold fact of life that she'd married for money.

"Okay...that's all I wanted to know."

She frowned. "Exactly what does that mean?"

"Nothing. Just that you knew about Sherman's little group. You knew about the wild parties, but didn't mention it. Why?"

She shrugged. "Was it important?"

"I think so."

"Well...if it was...then you found out. I gave you the list of names, didn't I? Well, why don't you look at it my way. I figure the less you know, the better. Maybe you'll find out something more than if I told you all. Where would you be, then?"

"Right where I am now, but quicker."

She sighed and stood. "I don't see what more we have to talk about."

"Where were you last night?"

"At home, in bed with my husband! Now, do you have any more questions?" she fired back.

"Yes, one! Where can I get hold of Phil Baxtar. I think you could tell me where he is."

She laughed. "Everybody wants to know where Phil Baxtar is. He's split. Out of the picture. Has been for several months. He's nowhere near the United States."

"How do you know?"

"I have letters to prove it! Mailed from Hong Kong, Japan, Germany. The last one was dated three days ago from England. One before that, the week before...before Linda was murdered he was in Spain."

"Why?"

"Ever hear of a vacation?"

"I mean, why did he write to you?"

"A natural thing. Considering that he'll be my son-in-law." She seemed suddenly ruffled.

"Maybe. Mind if I see one of those letters?"

"You may not!" she snapped angrily.

I considered her mood, and then decided against pushing. But I'd hit a nerve; maybe an important one.

She glared back at me and then suddenly said:

"I don't know if I want you to continue on this. I don't like your attitude, or your implications! In fact, you can go to hell!"

With that, Ann Harryington stomped out of the room.

I watched her leave, suddenly aware that I'd been quite completely fired. And in a way a sense of relief soothed over me.

As I got into my car a few moments later, the soothing relief continued to build. Then I remembered Sherman's offer of five grand to find the killer of Mary Jenkins, and another emotion ebbed through me.

I'd been fired by one client, but there was another to consider.

Starting the car, I decided to call it a day and headed for a restaurant to settle the sudden gnawing in my stomach.

Another decision formed in my tired brain. I remembered Sherry Anderson, her naked body, the offer she had so brazenly made.

The next hours killed themselves, first at a bar and then at a steak house, where I had a good helping of food to soften the effects of the booze, and washed that down with some more booze.

Then, by the time it was about 10:30, I drove out towards Vermont and 50th Street, and headed east until I came to a small strip joint labeled

THE HOT SPOT

Parking, I got out of the car and walked into the club.

It was dimly lighted, and the blast of a sax, drum and piano pounded at my ears the moment I walked inside.

A waitress in tight fitting skirt and blouse came up and asked: "Would you like to sit at the bar, or around the stage?"

I told her the stage, deciding to get a good show.

One of the strippers was onstage, a flat-chested broad who attempted to make up for the lack of breasts by hammering away with her hips. It was a sexual action dance, but had no emotion behind it. Finally she stripped to the stars and loin g-string and wiggled herself off the stage. After that a tall red-head took command. She was built like she didn't know where to stop.

"Miss Gloria Bombs!" the announcer said over the P.A. system.

I'd consumed a couple of Scotches and was working on my third as she started peeling off the clothing.

She had breasts that hung so long that it was easy to understand why somebody shouted: "Don't step on them, honey!"

Gloria Bombs smiled at him and wiggled her hips provocatively.

Her dance was a series of grinds and bumps designed to wiggle and jiggle her large, hanging breasts.

Finally, she finished off with revealing all that the law allowed.

"Miss Sherry Anderson, the Tigress Lady!"

Sherry was dressed in a tight-fitting leopard designed dress that hugged every voluptuous curve of her oversized body. But she looked magnificent. Cheap, but sexually exciting. It took her several circles around the stage before she spotted me sitting there at the ringside. Her smile was all honest sex, aimed directly at me. Her eyes seemed to light up into a vivid brightness of wanton desire.

Her routine was good enough to keep my full attention. Maybe it seemed so damned exciting to watch because I'd come so close to really making the point with the lady. Her breasts bounced beautifully, flowing easily with her graceful body movements.

Her hips ground and hammered, they pushed out in front of me, and she did a private little show that only the two of us were aware had any more promise in it than it might have if she'd done the same with another customer.

After she'd stripped down to blue stars and g-string, she fairly leaped off the stage, disappearing through the curtain.

"That's all for a few minutes ladies and gents," the announcer said. "We'll be back for a full show of more grind, bump and peak, in a little while. How about giving the ladies a big hand! And I bet you guys out there really would like to do just that!" The man's hands pumped and squeezed the air in front of his chest as his face contorted into a knowingly evil grin that brought on a burst of laughter from the audience.

Knowing that the star stripper is about to make a personal appearance at your table can do things to a man.

I waited, nervously, and then suddenly the waitress came up to me leaning over, and said, "Miss Sherry Anderson asked to have you come back stage."

I nodded, finished off my drink, left a ten dollar bill and then stood and said, "Bring back a couple of drinks."

I walked around to an entrance that said:

PRIVATE
NO ADMITTANCE

Which, of course, I completely ignored.

A big, muscular guy suddenly leaped out of nowhere and said, "What you want, mister?"

"Miss Anderson gave me the word. Where's her dressing room?"

He grinned, it was a leering grin. I wanted to punch it off. "That's the way, first door to your left. Have fun!"

I walked past him and then up to the door that was unmarked. I knocked.

"Yes?"

"Maxton."

"Come on in," Sherry's voice invited. I opened the door and found myself staring at a semi-nude woman. Sherry was still dressed in the g-string but the blue stars had disappeared. She sat at a dressing table, but facing the door. She smiled and stood as I closed the door behind me.

"Well, how'd you like the show?"

"Pretty exciting."

"Surprised to see you. Business or...pleasure?" she asked, looking seriously at me.

"Pleasure, I hope. Thought maybe I could drive you home tonight."

She grinned. The fire in her eyes was bright hot flame. "How nice," she offered after a moment, in an amused voice. "Via your apartment?"

"Why not?"

"Why not, for sure!" she laughed. Then she suddenly stepped forward and came into my arms. "I must say it took you some time to get around to me."

Strangely, she seemed a little less harsh, a little less common. Maybe that was because of the way her hips were pressing against mine, the way her lips finally leaned closer.

There just wasn't anything to do but kiss her. And the kiss was as wild as might have been expected, making full play of our tongues and bodies.

After a moment I said: "Maybe we better stop that before it goes too far!"

"It'll never be too far...not with me!" she promised.

There was a knock on the door and then it opened. "Your drinks," the woman said who had been waiting on me at the table.

"Thanks." When the waitress had left, I handed one of the drinks to Sherry who gulped down the Scotch in two large swallows.

"How much longer do you have to stay

around?" I asked.

"Just another hour, then I'm finished." We sat down on a small couch in the corner and just looked at one another for a long time.

Then suddenly we weren't looking at one another any more. The sight of her naked breasts, her flat stomach, was just too damned much to just sit there and look. Especially knowing they were mine to hand and to hold for the mere reaching out.

I pulled her into my arms and we rediscovered each other's mouths. After a long time she pushed away. "The door, lock it!"

No second orders were written. I stood, locked the door and then returned to Sherry, who had now removed her g-string and was reposed on the couch in a very inviting position.

It was only a matter of a few quick actions to strip. My clothing piled up on the chair and then I turned and stepped to the couch and then suddenly was in her soft, hot, yielding arms.

After having seen this woman semi-nude and completely naked twice before, and now an open offering to my caresses and kisses, I found it impossible to simply devour the banquet of her body. I simply wanted to consume it whole. My hunger had been built to a starvation level and now it was feast to eat time.

Caress led to caress, kiss led to kiss. My hands moved over her flesh, finding the yielding hallows and swells that fairly trembled under my circling fingers. She was a voluptuous sea of passion that moved under me with such controlled willing action, it was like we were meant for each other. I learned in those moments how good a stripper can

117

be. A stripper keeps her body in perfect shape, she can move with grace and with savage, violent rhythm. She went through all the actions a woman could go through, and then some.

The angry emotions that had driven me to the Hot Spot for just such late night action, blasted away at this voluptuous stripper until they were momentarily spent out.

It all happened fast, so fast that there was no doubt that it was merely a sampling to what would follow later in the night.

Afterwards I stood, and dressed, feeling better, less angry, less emotionally exhausted.

"You're pretty good, Stan," she observed. "I'll be looking forward to a real deal in an all night session." She laughed and then squeezed my arm. "After the show?"

"After the show," I promised, stepping toward the door and unlatching it.

I was pretty high by the time 1:30 came along and Sherry Anderson did her last strip and left the stage. Fifteen minutes later she was settling down beside me. We ordered a round of drinks and sat there talking and finishing them off. Finally we stood and left.

The excitement of her last act was still bubbling through my veins. She had put on a red dress this time and every action, every movement had been aimed at me. She teased a slow first number, just inching her dress off, and then later, during the faster tempo, whipped her hips into fiery bumps and grinds designed to fire up all the basic animal drives into hot flames throughout my body.

It had all left me at a high pitch of need. The

118

idea of spending the night with this wiggling ball of energy was almost overwhelming. All the way to the apartment she sat very close, her thigh against mine, as she smoked one cigarette after another.

Once the car was parked in the garage, we didn't waste any time getting into the apartment and the moment the door was closed behind us, she came hungrily into my arms.

The kiss fired the already raw nerves into blazing flame. My kiss probed deep into her mouth, searching, as she tensed against me, and as her mouth pulled on the kiss.

I was just reaching around to the back of her dress, to unzip it, when the phone started ringing. The sound jarred at my ears like explosions.

"Ignore it," she pleaded, wiggling against me.

I tried to do as she said, but the ringing continued.

Sighing, I released Sherry and moved to the phone, across the room.

Picking up the receiver, I shouted in an angry voice: "Yes?"

"Stan Maxton?" It was a feminine voice, slightly muffled, excited.

"Yes?"

"This is Dora Norton. I have to see you, right away. Can you come over here, now?"

She sounded frightened, desperate. "What is it?"

"It's important. I have to talk to you. I can't, over the phone! It's about Mary Jenkins' and Linda's death. I think I know who did it." For only a moment I hesitated, looking at Sherry. "I'll be right over."

Without saying goodbye, I slammed the receiver

on the hook.

"Dora Norton," I explained. "She knows who did the murders."

Sherry looked alarmed. "Can I go with you?"

"No." I started to say I'd drive her home, but remembered how far out she lived. "Look, honey, get a cab, I'm sorry about this...some other time?"

She smiled, shrugged.

"That a promise?"

I walked up to her, kissed her lips and said: "A promise you can be sure I'll keep."

With that, I rushed out of the apartment.

CHAPTER XI.

The drive to Dora Norton's place in North Hollywood was an agony of painfully counted minutes. Finally I pulled up into her driveway, slipped from behind the driver's seat and rushed to the porch.

The house was dark, and there wasn't a sound coming from it.

A warning bell clicked as I realized the front door was unlatched, and opened a fraction of an inch.

Frantically I pushed the door open, stepped into the darkness of the small living room. I was trying to get my eyes used to the blackness surrounding me when a soft, padded movement sounded from behind me.

Like I said in the beginning: act first, ask questions afterwards.

Only thing, there wasn't any time. Something hit the back of my head. I was still spinning around when the second blow slammed into the side of my face, knocking me down into a darker pool of nothingness that surged around me like a sick ebbing force, taking away all thought, all sensation, all worries.

A light was shining in my face. At first I couldn't remember what had happened last, or where I was. It was like coming out of a dreamless sleep of eternity, if you know what I mean. Confusion and then suddenly, like being slapped in the face, I remembered, groaned and moved.

My jaw was aching, the back of my head sore, but beyond that all seemed to be in fairly good order. That is, until I opened my eyes and saw my surroundings.

It was the same room I'd been in earlier; but a bit of a change had taken place.

One was the half-naked body of the young, beautiful woman I had come to see. Even in death she looked quite lovely.

She was stripped from the waist up, blood was smeared over her breasts and caked at a point just under her heart where the bullet apparently had gone in.

For a stunned moment I stood there, dazed, sick. Normally, death doesn't have that much of an effect on me. But this one did. She was so lovely, too lovely to have died, too young and alive. I hardly knew Dora Norton, except for that one short conversation, but she'd had an automatic reaction on me. Maybe it was merely because she was a woman, young and beautiful, that made me sick to the stomach. I turned away from the sight, raised my hands in front of my face, as if in an attempt to blot out the death scene.

A frosted chill straightened my back.

My hands were covered with blood. Automatically I guessed the reason and checked my clothing.

They were smeared with blood, too. The first reaction was to get the hell out of there, and fast! This time, someone had picked me out for a first class framing job and all the police had to do was hang me on the wall! The second instinctive slot my mind fell into was to be more thoughtful about what I did.

First: Dora had called me up. To that point she was alive. Possibly by gun-point, or by fact, what she had said to me was true. She had guessed who had killed Mary Jenkins and possibly therefore, Linda Harryington.

If that were true, there might just be some evidence that could lead me on the right track. But where to look?

Maybe the phone. I went there, throwing papers around on the floor, tossing away anything that might be of no use. I studied the phone book, but found nothing of interest. Then I looked at the doodle pad that had been next to the phone. My number was on it and several little markings, none of which made any sense, mere circles and frames. On impulse, I pocketed the pad and then started through Dora's purse I found in the living room on the floor by the television set.

There was lipstick, matches, which I pocketed, not even bothering to look at them, a couple of pieces of paper with writing on them that I also pocketed. There were keys and several other knick-knacks women keep in their purses for emergencies. A pack of cigarettes and a small, snub-nosed revolver.

That I pocketed.

I was just about to search elsewhere when the sound of a siren started swelling in the distance.

I didn't need a second warning. My fingers dropped the purse and I rushed out across the living room and into the kitchen, trying to find a back exit. There was a door leading to the garage. I took that and found myself in front of a small old Ford. There was another doorway across the garage. In the darkness I managed to make my way there just as the siren came to a dead silence outside the house.

I opened the door, peeked out.

A voice called at the front door. Then I heard the door open and footsteps walk into the house.

That's when I got the hell out of there, going across the back yard and down an alley. I kept running for all I was worth for well past five blocks. I came to a pay phone and was considering getting a cab when I remembered my clothing being covered with blood.

Somebody had taken a lot of time to fix me up good. That could only mean one thing: I was getting very close and didn't know it.

But right then I didn't care a damn about that. The first thing was to get as far away from that location as possible, and not be spotted. It was one of those kinds of messes that seem impossible to escape at the time. Yet, there was only one thing I could do: continue to hope for the best. While keeping on the move.

First thing, I found a gas station and came up on it from behind and sneaked into the men's room, praying that there wouldn't be anybody in there.

It took something like ten minutes to wash off the signs of blood from my shirt and jacket. I only bothered with those parts showing when the jacket was buttoned.

124

Then I left the men's room and went to a phone booth on the corner. Ten minutes later I was sitting in the back of a cab, driving toward my apartment. It wasn't until we were almost there that it occurred to my still numbed mind that the police would have, by now, put together a pretty clear picture of what they thought had happened. And that would point to me! And that would link the other two murders on me, too. This time motive would fly out the window; they wouldn't take any chances.

I looked at the cabby and said: "Changed my mind, take me to the Mayfair Hotel."

The next hours would be the telling ones. If I could possibly keep away from the police, maybe, just maybe, I could link together everything I knew about Linda and Mary and Dora, and figure out who killed them. I'd been framed in the last one for a very special reason: because I was getting too close for somebody's comfort. The cabby left me at the Mayfair Hotel and I walked into the lobby, stood there for a moment, giving the taxi driver a chance to drive away, and then left.

I walked for a long, long time, until I came to a crummy hotel on Main Street. There I got a room, locked myself in and emptied my pockets.

I arranged on the bed the phone pad, matches and the pieces of paper with writing on them. Studying the phone pad, it took only a few moments to decide it was a blank. Whatever Dora had found out, she hadn't unconsciously written down any hint that I could use. The matches stood out like a sore thumb. The Hot Spot. Two of the papers were merely personal notes, phone numbers with names; no names that I had heard of. The third piece of pa-

125

per had Sherry Anderson's phone number, address and a 4:30 written down on it. I looked at it and then shrugged. Nothing.

I threw my legs over onto the bed and stretched out, my hands behind my neck. Staring up at the ceiling I attempted to think out what had happened so far, what I'd learned that might possibly give me a clue, a clue that the murder seemed to think I possessed, or was close enough to possessing.

Linda Harryington had been killed in the beach house. Stabbed to death. She had told me she had an appointment that night, so that she couldn't spend it all with me. She ended up, or returned, to the beach house. In the early morning she'd apparently been killed.

Indication of a lover and a fight. But then why had she picked up with me? Why had she returned to the beach house to have another fling with another man?

That didn't seem reasonable, even considering her apparent healthy interest in bed games.

Fact one: she was rich. Some of her friends, in the group, were rich. The others were struggling to make ends meet, some pretty well off. A cross section.

Fact two: she played the field, all men were in that field, regardless of their possible attachment to another woman.

Fact three: all the people in the immediate gang seemed to quite freely change partners around, and didn't seem to mind. That would, apparently, cut out the jealous killer tag.

Fact four: she and her step-mother were old friends.

Suddenly I remembered the letters Ann Harryington had received from Phil Baxtar—letters she refused to let me see. Why?

No answer that was reasonable, unless Ann and Phil had been lovers. But that shouldn't have bothered Linda. Ann was also balling it with Larry Sherman before her marriage with Harryington. But, apparently, she had stopped the affair with Larry once she married her husband. Why had she dropped Sherman? He had money, or at least seemed to have a lot of money. Did she stop because she really loved Ralph Harryington? Then why was she having an affair with Phil Baxtar, if she was?

That was a dead end.

I dropped that line of reasoning. Returned to listing facts.

Fact five: Linda got kicks out of posing nude. She let the pictures be published. She didn't charge Jay Eaton anything for posing for him. Implication was that she'd been having an affair with Jay. Logical enough, all things considered.

Fact six: publisher Peters had a thing for Linda. His son knew nothing about Linda's frantic sex life, he was merely a friend, and nothing more.

Fact seven: Mary Jenkins, having talked to me, then after having completed her pass, left in a sudden hurry. Had something been said between the two of us to suggest to her who might have killed Linda? If so, why had she gone to Larry Sherman's place? What had they talked about that night? Where did that fit in? Or did it?

I was going around in circles, like a rat in a maze. Questions but no answers.

I backed up. Decided to work it another way. Start with a motive and attempt to discover a person who would fit into the motive.

Jealousy. That would list Frank Peters and Jay Eaton on top. But it would also list almost any other person in the group, man or woman.

What other motive? Linda was rich. Some of the cats in the group were rubbing pennies together.

Blackmail?

Who then? What kind of blackmail? Why?

Motive: money. Means: her wild life. No, that wouldn't sound too reasonable.

Motive: money. Means: pictures were usually the reason for blackmail, something solid that could be used to prove the point to somebody. The papers? Her father? Phil Baxtar?

Person! Who was more logical than Jay Eaton? He took pictures. He was a struggling photographer. He had a temper.

One solid suspect.

I sat up in bed, suddenly alert.

Jay Eaton was a number one suspect. Temper. Means. Reason. Motive.

Linda had returned to the beach house that night, and it didn't seem reasonable it would have been for a lover. Blackmail. A man had been seen by a witness running out of the house in the early morning.

The conversation with Mary Jenkins must have sparked her mind, must have given her a clue. Suddenly I wished there was a tape recording of that conversation. Mary Jenkins ran to Sherman. Why was Mary killed?

I stood and decided to work one murder at a

time. Once a hole had been made in the dike, the walls would come tumbling down.

Leaving the hotel room, I went down to the lobby, called for a cab and a little later was being driven to Jay Eaton's apartment.

The more I thought about my conclusions, the surer I was that I'd hit upon the solution of the case.

When the taxi stopped, I paid the cabby and leaped out, rushed into the large building and then slammed to a stop. A policeman was standing in the lobby, idly reading.

For a moment I stood there, unsure of what to do, then I turned and slowly walked out, across the street and into a darkened doorway of a shop.

I waited for some time before the sound of a siren broke the night stillness. A few moments later an ambulance pulled up in front of the apartment house. Two men in white got hurriedly out and disappeared into the apartment, carrying a stretcher. About ten minutes later they returned, a man was lying on the stretcher and a couple of police followed after the men in white. A moment later Lt. Hanson and Captain Turner, my friend in the Hollywood police force, stepped out onto the street.

I didn't have to guess who it was that had been put in the ambulance. I waited until everybody had left the scene and then slowly I moved from the doorway, still stunned, still as far away from the solution as I'd been at the beginning.

Four murders. Three women and now Jay Eaton. That threw my theories to hell and back.

Then I suddenly reconsidered. One: Jay Eaton apparently wasn't dead yet. Why had someone tried to kill him? Take my reasoning about blackmail and

I could come up with a partner. But who? A partner who got scared and tried to kill Eaton to keep him quiet. That made the partner the top gun, the brains. Then another thought hit me. It had taken money to hire two thugs to work me over. I'd almost forgotten that. Money means a man of some position; some authority. Who?

Larry Sherman had money; he might have had reason to kill Linda, but not Mary, his niece.

But what if for some reason something had gone wrong? What if Sherman didn't have all the money he claimed to have, what if he was on the verge of going bankrupt? What if he had been blackmailing Linda with photos, that he threatened to take either to her father or Phil Baxtar, or the papers, and then accidentally killed her? What if his niece guessed the truth and then he was forced to kill her? Would his blood-love be that strong?

Suddenly I knew I was grasping at a straw. But an idea occurred to me. All I had to do was attempt to find out Sherman's financial situation to prove or disprove that theory.

At least it would eliminate a theory one way or another.

I remembered another factor: Ann Harryington's sudden dropping of Sherman and picking up with Harryington. If she were the gold digger I'd suspected, then there could only be one reason.

Time was against me. I had to risk a bluff. If Sherman wasn't the man, maybe he could possibly give me a lead. After all, I was working for him, not Ann Harryington now.

It was only a matter of getting another cab and driving out to Bel Air and seeing Sherman.

130

CHAPTER XII.

The butler was in a bathrobe and a little brisk when I asked to see Larry Sherman.

"What's the meaning of disturbing Mr. Sherman at this late hour?" the man demanded in an irritated voice.

"Tell him that Stan Maxton is here to see him."

"At this hour of..."

"It's important. Tell him I think I know who killed his niece."

That got the reaction I expected. The butler let me in and told me to wait in the drawing room.

I waited for something like ten minutes and then Larry Sherman came into the large, period furnished living room, a morning robe around him.

His eyes looked bloodshot and the expression on his face was angry.

"What is it this time?" he demanded. "You better have a good story. I don't like being disturbed at night."

He didn't extend his hand, but merely stood there in the middle of the room.

I waited for a moment and then said: "I understand your financial situation is buckling under you." My voice had been so mild, so casual that it seemed to take the man several moments to adjust to what I'd dropped in his face like a bomb.

He stared at me for a moment, his expression blank. Then he turned, walked to an end table, opened a cigar box, lighted one of the stogies and then slowly turned and faced me.

"What makes you think that?" he said in a soft, careful voice.

"A little investigation in the right places." He sat there on the sofa, tense, ready for any kind of action about to be played out.

"So...I've run into a little choppy water. What of it?" Sherman admitted. "You'll get paid in any case."

"I wasn't worried about that, so much." I stood, braced myself on spread feet, ready to spring into action, if something suddenly exploded.

"Jay Eaton was taken to the hospital this evening," I told him in a conversational voice.

"What happened to him?" Sherman asked.

"Somebody tried to kill him, from what I understand. But the police say he'll be okay...and be able to tell who tried to kill him!"

The last I spit out at him like a gun shot.

Larry Sherman shrugged. "What's that got to do with Mary's death?"

"I think he had some pictures he was blackmailing Linda with. I think there was somebody behind him, who was the brains. I think that Mary Jenkins was killed because she guessed who the brains were. I think I person with brains had to have money, enough to hire a couple of hoods to work me over the other day. I also think that Phil Baxtar is in the United States and—"

Sherman laughed. It was a low, amused sound. "Next thing you'll be telling me is that Baxtar is the…'brains'…like you call it."

"Not quite!" Suddenly a thought jarred me; a thought so startling and out of left field that I couldn't really buy it at first. It shot to hell the theory of blackmail, but took into account two other facts. One: that Phil Baxtar had returned to the States after Linda's death, logical thing, considering they were engaged to be married, even if there wasn't any real love lost between them. Two: Ann Harrington had refused to let me see the Baxtar letters she claimed to have received from different parts the world. Add that together, and mix it with the fact that Ann and Larry Sherman had been lovers before she'd married Harrington, and I came to a startling conclusion.

"I think Baxtar is dead!" I blurted out.

The expression on Sherman's face was like he'd been slapped by a sledge hammer His eyes narrowed, his lips tightened the cigar, every muscle seemed to tense.

"I think that Baxtar found out about you and Ann and was about to tell Harryington and you killed him and Linda found out, and you had to kill her, then…" I'd talked myself out of a theory. It didn't seem reasonable that Jay Eaton would have found out, or been killed.

The relief on Sherman's face revealed that I'd gone too far to the left. But I'd come close enough.

He turned and said: "Really, Maxton, you have an imagination, but I think you're a little too involved now..." Suddenly he turned and there was a revolver in his hand.

"Since the police figure you murdered Dora Norton, on which they've put out a bulletin for your arrest, and they'll connect you up with Linda's and Mary's death, maybe we might as well come out in the open about this! It's about time you were silenced for good." He made a motion with the gun. "Sit down, detective man."

Slowly, carefully, I sat, puzzled more than frightened.

"To begin with, you were pretty close in the beginning. Baxtar is dead. He had found out about our little business activities...and didn't buy. You see, Jay and myself were in on a pretty sweet arrangement. The parties here were a front for what was actually going on. I'd get guys like Baxtar in bed with some girl and Jay would take pictures with high speed film. When I made my play for Baxtar...well, he merely laughed at me. Said he couldn't be touched.

"But what was far more worse...the woman with him was Ann Harryington and he merely laughed at me, and suggested that I tell the whole world about it! His added remark pushed me too far. Either I told the whole world, or he would! Baxtar was a real first class bastard. He had enough money to buy and sell the city of Los Angeles and not even feel it. That was my mistake. I'll admit that. I didn't have any choice but to kill him. Then it was necessary to develop a cover story. We just made Phil take a trip! That was one thing nice about Phil, he had a habit of disappearing for long periods of time, and being so rich, very few people knew much about him.

"The trouble was that Linda happened to drop by that evening, and we had to kill her. It was my idea of driving her to the beach house. You see, Linda had expected that Ann was seeing me, and she, strangely enough, didn't like the idea of her step-mother having an affair with another man. Linda was a strange woman...a lush and bitch on one side, but she tried to do a lot of good for those around her, like her writer pick-up, and ironically enough for Jay Eaton, who didn't need the help, but that had been a good cover for him, too.

"It was only by accident that you came into the picture, having been her last lover. We got nervous about that, but Ann played a smart one. Having you put on the case would at least do one of two things: either you'd find out who killed Linda, or get yourself more involved."

His expression changed a little.

"I didn't like killing Mary...we were good pals. But pals are one thing and love another. Mix that up with murder and there really wasn't any choice. Apparently you had said something to her that night that got her to thinking and she came here and accused me of killing Linda. She hadn't guessed the real reasons, but she said she would go to the police and was giving me enough time to get out of town, lost, in other words. Sweet choice. Just like in those television westerns: the town is just too small for both of us...so you get on your way, buddy."

He laughed at that in real humor.

"Dora was an ad-lib. I merely arranged to have her held, Ann did the actual calling...you fell into that one beautifully. You see, Dora got wise to Jay's little business...how, I'll never know. But Eaton started getting scared. I guess I didn't do a very good job on him, but..."

He motioned with the gun again.

"Get up, we're going to have a little fight, of course you won't actually have anything to do with it. But you'll be killed and I don't think I'll make a mistake with you!"

CHAPTER XIII.

I realized suddenly that I was facing death. But death didn't know that I had two advantages over him. One, the .38 snub-nosed revolver in my jacket pocket I'd taken from Dora Norton's purse, and second: the desperation of a doomed man. I had nothing to lose. He had everything to lose.

Advantage or not, life is a beautiful thing no man wants to end one instant sooner than possible. You look at that bored hole in the middle of the barrel and all you can think of is when will death come spitting out?

"Would you mind...a cigarette and a few questions first?" I inquired. "After all, you have it all your way, there's nothing to lose by giving me a few moments longer to live."

He smiled, one of those pleased, sadistic smiles to light up his whole face. The smile was generous. "Why not?"

The gun didn't waiver. It was pointed at my gut, a place where a bullet can do a lot of damage and take its time eating away your life with a slow, painful death.

"What'd you want to know?" he asked pleasantly.

"Several things aren't quite clear. One is: why did Ann marry Ralph Harryington?"

"No reason not to! Ralph's a charming man! And he has all that money...he offered marriage."

"Why didn't you?"

"Oh, come on, I've lived too long my own life to want to get married! Ann's a sweet girl, but nothing more!" He laughed. "Actually, she was pretty taken with me, but well, that's an old story! Maybe it's good she was. She liked kicks, and she liked the idea of taking rich men for a dollar. Ann never really got used to being rich. I met her a long time before Linda did, though Linda never knew. When Mrs. Harryington died, I suggested she enter college, she'd done two and a half years before.

"The point was to make friends with Linda, who was a sweet little kind of girl then, shy. Some time later she met a guy who made her really flip. Father Harryington put the brakes on that and well, sent her to Europe for a spell. She never got over that, yet strangely...she was attached to her old man. Like I said, that's why she came over to the house. Apparently she'd been with you to kill time, and planned on catching Ann and myself in bed together.

"Actually, she caught us with a dead body on our hands." He smiled thinly. "Dora was balling it with Eaton and saw some pictures and asked about them, and then one question led to another, I understand, and she accused him of killing Linda, and he yelled to me, I had to do the only thing possible. Kill her, and pin it on you."

"What makes you believe the police will think I

138

did it?"

"Oh, come on, your finger prints are all over the place. Plus, it was your gun that fired the shot. We arranged for that, too! Actually, we broke in with a skeleton key and searched for anything to serve as a weapon. Eaton was with me, then.

"After we left you at Dora's place, we just went to his apartment, all the time he was nervous, chattering. It was the first killing he'd been an actual part of. Well, he was just too nervous...so, I did what was necessary and rushed home, got undressed and went to bed. You came along...and, here we are!"

His face hardened. "Enough of this!"

"Wait, the cigarette you promised!" I quickly said, holding up my hands.

He shrugged, but irritation showed on his face. I thought about Eaton, and the fact that the man knew a lot about what was happening. If he lived, he would be my only link to proving that Sherman was lying. But if I were dead, it wouldn't do much good.

I reached into my coat pocket, as if to pull out a pack of cigarettes. The chances of my getting away with this were pretty slim.

"How many murders do you think you can get away with?" I asked, casually.

"This, I believe, should be my last, considering it won't be necessary any more. After all, they'll think you did it!"

His smile broadened as my fingers clutched onto the .38 revolver.

"I wouldn't do that, if I were you!" he announced. "Pull your hand slowly out...and don't make one simple move."

My amazement must have shown on my face. What did I have to lose?

He said: "Naturally I noticed the bulky weight in your pocket and—"

I squeezed the trigger and dived to one side as a second shot rang out through the room. I felt searing pain cut into my left shoulder.

I rolled, twisted and pulled the gun from my pocket, aimed and fired, just as something kicked the back of my neck. It was a sharp pointed shoe.

The blackness blurred away and I heard voices. Apparently I hadn't been unconscious for more than a couple of minutes.

Ann Harryington's voice was speaking. "...and I came over the moment I heard the news flash about Eaton."

"It's a good thing," Larry Sherman said in a painful voice. "I just thank God I gave you that key."

"What are we going to do?" she pleaded in anguish.

"We'll have to wait and see if Eaton survives, and then...I don't know," Sherman's voice said worriedly.

"What about him?"

"That's a problem."

There was a short silence, then Sherman said: "I'd planned on killing him...but now I don't know quite how to go about it. If Eaton says anything to the police, we've had it. There's really no point, I thought he was bluffing about Eaton being merely wounded. I was so damned sure I'd finished Eaton off. The bullet went right into his heart, I would have sworn."

140

"They say in the left lung, just a fraction from his heart," Ann said. "What are we going to do? This has become a terrible mess. I never thought it would end like this, Larry. We should get the hell out of here...before it's too late."

I'd managed to keep from moving all this time, even to keeping my eyes shut. Now I sensed that there might be a chance of getting out of this situation; how, I wasn't quite sure. At least I'd been given a breather; and a breather could mean the difference between life and death.

Sherman sighed, and said: "Maybe that's not a bad idea at that. Disappear until we find out how things are...we'll have to take this bright boy with us, in the event that Eaton dies—we kill him, call the police and then sit pretty. If Eaton lives, we kill him and get the hell out of the country. I have enough money stashed away in the safe, here, to take care of us for awhile."

I heard footsteps move toward me; heavy male footsteps. Every muscle in my body readied itself.

A foot touched my ribs, pushing, in an attempt to turn me over on my back. Then I moved, wrapping my good right arm around the leg and jerking with all my strength.

Sherman gave out a yell and slammed to the floor as I leaped to my feet. There wasn't any time for polite fair play. I kicked with my right foot, smashing it into the side of Sherman's head before the man could recover from the surprise attack. The impact was hollow sounding as the man slumped against the floor, unconscious.

Turning, I faced Ann Harryington. And the revolver in her hand.

"Don't!" she warned.

After a moment to catch my breath and attempt to feel out some plan of action, I said: "Why don't you put that thing down. You couldn't use it on me, anyway!"

"Don't try me!" she warned, stiffening, her face drawn and white, her eyes large with fear.

There was about five feet between us. Too far to attempt a lunge, I thought, and thought fast.

"Look, Ann, you aren't as involved as Sherman. If Eaton lives, you've had it, and you know it. You can't run far enough for the authorities. And once they get at you...it's the end. Sherman will turn on you like a snake."

"What good would that do him?" she demanded, laughing. But it was a forced laugh.

"You don't really think he gives a damn about you, do you? Hell, if Eaton dies, all he has to do is dump you in the nearest river and be free as a bird, for life! Nobody will know a thing Everyone involved will have been killed and he'll get away with it. Look at Eaton."

I was merely playing for time and ad-libbing as fast as the words would come. "*If* he'd really cared a damn about you—why'd he let you marry Harrington?"

She squinted at me and the humor left her face.

"Look, if you give me that gun, and turn yourself in, tell the police what really happened, you have a good chance to get off with a life sentence. From what he told me, you didn't actually commit any of the murders"

"What if Eaton lives?"

"He'll name you both. You don't have much

142

time to beat him to it, do you?" I was sweating, my hand near the point of shaking. The pain in my left shoulder was beginning to grow and the world was fuzzy around the edges.

"We'll run!" she pointed out.

"And won't Sherman dump you at the first chance? He likes to play his women wide, likes a lot of them. If you got in the way, out you'd go, feet first...dead!"

Her eyes shot to Sherman and I leaped. I was gambling on the fact that her reflexes would be slowed by the suspicions I'd put in her mind.

My hand lanced out for the gun, my body lunged against hers. What happened exactly in those last moments I'm not quite sure. She had the advantage of two hands, but I had strength and weight. The latter won out.

I managed to twist the gun from her hand and then forcefully shove her backwards into the chair behind her.

Moving quickly away, I leveled the gun at Ann.

For a moment the two of us glared at one another, then she burst into tears.

"Please, Stan...let me get away...please. I'll give you anything...anything at all. Myself. I'll say that Sherman killed all of them and that you..." Her voice broke off, apparently because of the hard, cold expression on my own face. After a moment she gained control of herself and straightened.

I moved across the room as far away as I could get from the two. Once Sherman was conscious, it wouldn't be a good idea to be too close to them.

I picked up the phone, but before dialing I said to Ann: "I'm calling the police, and believe me, it would be smart for you to tell them all you know...and right away, before you even find out that Eaton is dead or alive! You'll have one hell of a better chance that way, believe me!"

Her face didn't change expressions. It remained hard, defeated.

I dialed and waited for the operator. Then I said: "Give me the police station."

CHAPTER XIV.

We were stretched out on the bed, nude, enjoying the aftermath of one beautifully exhausting lovematch.

Sherry Anderson looked up at me and smiled that way a woman has when she is completely satisfied, but still will want more of the meal being served.

She looked magnificent. Her breasts were high on her chest, their rosy centers relaxed now, but still inviting, maybe even more inviting.

"What will happen to Ann Harryington?" she inquired, in a soft, almost sad voice.

"Probably life...which is better than nothing," I said, caressing one of her breasts.

She trembled and said: "I just don't understand how Larry could be like that!"

"Fanatic, a little overly used to life as a rich man. I understand that his company folded several years back. He had enough money to invest, but it turned sour...there just wasn't anything else for him to do but go out and earn an honest living, a point that didn't appeal to him. He knew enough cats who liked to live it up and got the idea of making use of it to give him a good income. He'd been giving the squeeze to several 'friends' for some time. They were willing to come forth, in private, anyway, and back up the story of his activities. How he lasted so long is the miracle. He made the mistake of pushing the wrong kind of guy. Baxtar had enough money to buy his way out of anything, and didn't like the idea of paying blackmail...at least that's what Ann said. She claimed the first killing was an accident. Larry Sherman apparently saw red when he was faced with exposure and...it just happened. They buried Baxtar's body in the hills above his house...then took Linda to the beach house, figuring that anybody who did try any investigation would believe the motive to be jealousy, which I did. When they learned about me, and the fact that I'd apparently spent the evening with her...well, it was easy to put me on the trail, and hope I'd go around in circles...and if I got too close...well...then do what they did! Mr. Harryington had been the one who saw to it that somebody was hired...Ann just hoped things would work out...somehow. Sherman had other plans, apparently, which in the end, he put to use. Framing me would be easy, under the circumstances."

I caressed the flat of her stomach, already tired of the conversation. The sight of her nudity was beginning to build the normal, healthy desire for party games.

Things had been pretty hectic in the last days.

That evening, between the times I'd called the police and they arrived, I had experienced a terrible agony of suspense. Sherman was conscious by the

146

time the law arrived and only with threats to use the gun had I been able to keep him from talking to Ann. I had her worried, and wanted to keep her that way. Then the law made the scene and I nodded to Ann, who started talking a blue streak, much to my relief.

Later I learned how close it had been. Eaton had died on the operating table without ever regaining consciousness.

After that there had been the statements, the questions and all the aftermath of tying up the loose ends for Lt. Hanson.

Now I was on my bedroom case spree, and didn't plan on spending any more time in talking business than was necessary.

My hand gripped hold of Sherry's shoulder.

"Let's go back to the other conversation we were having so much fun with!" I suggested with a thin smile spreading across my face.

Her frown questioned me.

"The physical conversation between our bodies. I have a lot more to say!"

Sherry laughed and slipped her arms around my neck.

After that, the conversation was hot and wild and much more satisfying than anything we'd said to each other before. This was the kind of conversation that could go on all night, and, in the end, we managed to communicate until late the next morning.

ABOUT THE AUTHOR

Charles Nuetzel was born in San Francisco in 1934, and writes:

"As long as I can remember I wanted to be a writer. It was a dream I never thought would materialize. But with the help of Forrest J Ackerman, who became my agent, I managed to finally make it into print.

"I was lucky enough not only in selling my work to publishers but also ending up packaging books for some of them, and finally becoming a 'publisher' much like those who had bought my first novels. From there it as a simple leap to editing not only a sci-fi anthology, but a line of sci-fi books for Powell Sci-Fi back in the 1960s. Throughout these active professional years I had the chance to design some covers and do graphic cover layouts for pocket books & magazines."

Much of his work in covers and graphics are a result of having had a father who was a professional commercial artist, and who did a number of covers for sci-fi magazines in the 1950s and later for pocket books—even for some of Mr. Nuetzel's books.

In retirement he has become involved in swing dancing, a long time lover of Big Band jazz. But more interestingly world travels have taken him (and his wife Brigitte) across the world, to Hawaii, Caribbean, Mexico, Kenya, Egypt, Peru, having a life-long interest in ancient civilizations. His website is full of thousands of pictures taken during these trips.